DARK RAGE

Skye Fargo came to in inky blackness, with a dull, pounding headache. He blinked his eyes and nothing happened. His eyelids seemed frozen, sewn shut. What was wrong?

Blood. That was it. The beating he had taken had gushed blood all around his eye sockets. The blood had congealed, gluing his eyelashes down. That made sense.

But after he mopped both eyes out with his bandanna, it didn't make any difference. Those bastards must have blinded him with their savage blows.

Blindness. Never to see another mountain sunset or a woman's smile. Never to find tracks or hunt game or . . .

Fargo stopped there. No way he could be blind. He'd find a way to see again. And even if didn't, he'd find a way to kill . . .

CAVE OF DEATH

by

Jon Sharpe

A SIGNET BOOK

NEW AMERICAN LIBRARY

A DIVISION OF PENGUIN BOOKS USA INC.

PUBLISHER'S NOTE

This book is a work of fiction. Names, characters, places, and incidents either are the product of the author's imagination or are used fictitiously, and any resemblance to actual persons, living or dead, events, or locales is entirely coincidental.

NAL BOOKS ARE AVAILABLE AT QUANTITY DISCOUNTS
WHEN USED TO PROMOTE PRODUCTS OR SERVICES.
FOR INFORMATION PLEASE WRITE TO PREMIUM MARKETING DIVISION,
NEW AMERICAN LIBRARY, 1633 BROADWAY,
NEW YORK, NEW YORK 10019.

The first chapter of this book previously appeared in *Mesabi Huntdown*, the ninetieth volume in this series.

SIGNET TRADEMARK REG. U.S. PAT. OFF. AND FOREIGN COUNTRIES
REGISTERED TRADEMARK—MARCA REGISTRADA
HECHO EN DRESDEN, TN, USA

SIGNET, SIGNET CLASSIC, MENTOR, ONYX, PLUME, MERIDIAN AND NAL BOOKS are published by New American Library, a division of Penguin Books USA Inc., 1633 Broadway, New York, New York 10019

First Signet Printing, July, 1989

1 2 3 4 5 6 7 8 9

PRINTED IN THE UNITED STATES OF AMERICA

The Trailsman

Beginnings . . . they bend the tree and they mark the man. Skye Fargo was born when he was eighteen. Terror was his midwife, vengeance his first cry. Killing spawned Skye Fargo, ruthless, cold-blooded murder. Out of the acrid smoke of gunpowder still hanging in the air, he rose, cried out a promise never forgotten.

The Trailsman, they began to call him, all across the West: searcher, scout, hunter, the man who could see where others only looked, his skills for hire but not his soul, the man who lived each day to the fullest, yet trailed each tomorrow. Skye Fargo, the Trailsman, the seeker who could take the wildness of a land and the wanting of a woman and make them his own.

July 1862, along the Arkansas River.
Once this was the headquarters of an empire,
but now the stench of decay masks the
odor of greed and savagery. . . .

1

Half a dozen men were wolfing down supper in the dining room of the stage station, but Señora María Teresa Espinoza y Vigil sat by herself. Her dark eyes sent unmistakable signals to only one—the tall broad-shouldered man with shoulder-length black hair, a full beard, and lake-blue eyes that returned the señora's provocative messages. Skye Fargo had just stopped in for a sit-down meal during a trek from Santa Fe to Denver, and he got the distinct impression that the lady was in a hurry. After finishing her dinner, she wasted no time as she sidled past him and whispered that he'd be a welcome visitor to her room.

Less than an hour later, the cotton chemise, aided by the Trailsman's nimble and eager fingers, dropped from Señora Espinoza's rounded shoulders. The plump but appealing woman sighed and stepped back a bit, giving Fargo a better view of her full breasts.

He had never seen a pair he didn't like, and hers looked damn good in this soft glow. The flickering and smoky tallow candle sat atop an iron holder that had been jammed into the adobe wall. Her tiny room, perhaps eight feet square, sat at a stage stop on the north bank of the Arkansas River, about seventy miles east of the Rocky Mountains.

The stage stop was still called Bent's Old Fort, in honor of William and Charles Bent, who had built it back in 1833. These days, however, much of the immense adobe castle was just ruins, melting back into the earth. What remained were a few sleeping rooms on each side of the old main gate, a kitchen and dining room, a smithy, and facilities for a few dozen mules, which outnumbered the people here by a considerable margin. But Jared Sanderson, the local manager for the Kansas City, Santa Fe & Canon City Fast Line, was trying hard: Señora Espinoza's room had a fresh coat of whitewash.

Doña María Teresa seemed to think she could use a fresh coat of paint too, and she stepped back a bit. She pouted pensively while Fargo's eyes sparkled and his generally serious expression lifted into the start of an appreciative grin. But that wasn't enough to improve her disposition.

"Alas," the short and roundish woman murmured, "the passing years are not as kind to women as they are to men."

Those candlelit highlights in her shoulder-length, raven-black hair might well have been small streaks of gray, perhaps her midsection had been a little flatter a few years ago, and maybe those luscious breasts did sag a bit, but Fargo didn't see any cause for complaint.

"No," he soothed, "beautiful women are like fine wine: they just get better with age." He was sure he'd said the right thing when her fingers returned to removing his shirt.

"It was most kind of you to say that, *señor*, even though you cannot really believe such a thing," she whispered while Fargo bent down, first cupping her breasts, then nuzzling her nipples until they grew to be as large as, and considerably sweeter than, the chokecherries that grew along the river.

Señora Espinoza sighed contentedly. Her strong hands began to knead Fargo's shoulder blades. He eased his own hands down the hollow of her back, to the top of her frilly drawers. He slid one hand below, to savor the swell of her firm rump.

She sighed again, but then shook her head. A bit of

determination crept into her round face, and she backed up so that one more step would put her atop the bed.

It wasn't the normal frame bed. It was more of a bench, made in a hollow of the thick adobe outer wall. A cornhusk mattress provided some comfort, and gaudy Navaho trade blankets served as the covers, which were hardly necessary on this August night. The room was sweltering, and Fargo felt even hotter, even though Doña María Teresa now seemed intent on cooling things.

"Oh, *señor*, what kind of woman do you take me for?" she teased.

"One who knows a good thing when she sees it," Fargo muttered, not really of a mind to talk. Getting his hands back under those drawers seemed a lot more important than any of this foolish chatter.

She batted her long dark lashes as Fargo straightened and pressed tight against her, just so she'd know that she had inspired a throbbing insistence that was growing by the minute.

"That is true, *señor*," she conceded, her voice husky. "But I am not a woman of haste."

During dinner, Fargo had listened halfheartedly to the woman's story of woe. It was a commonplace tale of petty complaints about the dusty and jarring stage ride that she had endured. Her lamentation ended with her abandonment at this stage station. Apparently, her man hadn't met her stage as planned. He was supposed to get her to their land, a hundred miles to the west, but whoever he was, he hadn't shown up by dinner, which meant he wasn't likely to appear before morning.

Although Fargo hadn't been attracted by the woman's petulant whine, he couldn't make himself ignore the rise and fall of her heavy bosom when she sighed out her story. He felt a surge of irritation as he recalled how hastily she had cajoled him to her room. He'd barely managed to finish dinner. And now she was saying that she wanted to take things slow and easy.

Well, as long as a man was enjoying what he was doing, there wasn't any cause for undue haste. Fargo took a deep breath of heat and tallow smoke. He slid his hands back around, staying atop those silk underthings this time. Through the smooth silk, he pressed and rubbed her jutting buttocks, which soon began a rhythmic motion of their own.

Before long, Doña María Teresa didn't mind that Fargo's probing hands were beneath the silk. So that she could pretend she didn't know what was going on, he proceeded slowly. His hands slid around to the outermost swell of her hips. He bowed his wrists so that the drawers slid down, then he eased down and repeated the process until her most interesting parts were within reach.

Out in the hard-packed yard under a rising full moon, some horses, along with a wagon or two, drew up amid the furious barking of the resident mongrels. Wafting in through the room's tiny window, the commotion inspired Doña María Teresa to move a little faster. Her fingers found the buttons of Fargo's fly. In what seemed but an instant, he was stepping out of his denim trousers.

With his patient help, her drawers had slipped down near her knees by that time. Embracing him tightly about the waist, as his shaft prodded against her soft navel, Doña María Teresa danced back. After confirming that the bed was right behind her, she lay back, pulling Fargo down atop her.

Now she was in a hurry. Her breath came in fevered gasps. She moved her hands down, as if to push him into her as her thighs spread wide and began to envelop him.

Fargo didn't need much encouragement. He plunged into her welcome moistness, pressing down as she arched up to meet him. Her bare feet, still planted on the woven mat next to the bed's niche, gave her enough leverage to ensure that their initial coupling was deep and complete.

That tremendous thrust was more than Doña María Teresa had planned on. "You are too much for me, *señor*," she protested, the words tumbling out in a frenzied mixture of English and Spanish.

Fargo knew better, as did the rest of her body, so he smothered further protests with a kiss and continued to thrust. She sidled, so as to get her feet off the floor, and Fargo went along with it. They were both atop the blankets, pounding away, when she started to shudder.

Her ankles locked over him and her plump thighs squeezed his hips with a bear-trap grip. Her hands rained little hammerlike blows on his back.

Fargo slid his hands off her shoulders, pressing them against the bed so he could lift his torso and slide into a more comfortable position—this bed had a wall at each end, and it had been built for shorter people.

Before settling back down, he enjoyed the view of her dark-eyed passion. Her rolling and heaving huge breasts were flushed from pressing against him. Her hips rose and fell, then rose again to grasp his submerged organ more tightly.

"Now, now," she urged. "Wait no longer."

Fargo didn't argue with her, but he didn't rush to cooperate, either. He settled back down against her so that every possible bit of her eager flesh was pressed against his. It was just what a man needed after a lonely week in the saddle, bound for no particular place.

What a man didn't need right now was an interruption, but one was coming. Fargo's sensitive ears heard padding footsteps outside, their sound barely audible above María Teresa's purr. He rolled across her, getting to his gun just as the door was kicked open, its flimsy latch flying across the room.

The angry man standing in the portal was dressed vaquero-style: polished boots with high heels and narrow toes, tight black twill trousers with some silver along the outer seams, a loose white cotton shirt with embroidered patterns, and a tremendous dark sombrero. His extensive mustache bristled and his eyes flashed in anger, which was something to consider, since he had a cocked revolver in his right hand.

"Unhand my wife, you gringo bastard," he announced.

"As you can see," Fargo replied from his naked crouch on the floor, "I don't have a hand, or anything else, on that woman."

When the man shifted his glare to confirm that, Fargo used the opportunity to silently bring up his own pistol. He kept it close to his right side, in the shade of his body where it wouldn't be seen.

"You have shamed me and destroyed my honor, *señor*," the intruder proclaimed. His voice dropped into a more polished baritone. "I, Ramón, her lawful husband—I demand satisfaction."

This wasn't the first time the Trailsman had been caught in the old badger game. Every footloose man got trapped occasionally, unless he was celibate.

A woman would act real available. Then she'd make it clear that her man wasn't around. You'd get to her room, she'd shed a few clothes, but before the fun started in earnest, her partner—sometimes, but not necessarily, her husband—would appear. He'd brandish a pistol and wail about his sullied honor. After he made his speech, he'd get around to settling for all the money you had on you.

If this had been the usual badger game, Fargo would have caught on instantly. But María Teresa and Ramón were working it with some new variations. She had been so caustic in her complaining that it was hard to believe she was experienced at luring men. If Fargo hadn't just been alone on a trail for a week, her whining would have chased him away. As the game was usually played, Ramón should have shown up just in time to save his and María Teresa's "honor."

Ramón must have been delayed tonight, or else María Teresa had been more eager than usual. Fargo sometimes had that effect on women.

Ramón's low voice interrupted Fargo's thoughts. "*Señor*, did you not hear me? I demand satisfaction."

"You want a duel? How about here and now?"

Ramón blanched at the speed with which a long-barreled Colt revolver materialized in the Trailsman's hand.

"*Señor*, perhaps there is a more sensible way to settle this outrage against my honor."

"Meaning that if I gave you a few double eagles, your honor would be satisfied?"

Ramón nodded.

"That's too much," Fargo protested. "A plugged nickel would be too much for your honor. You're nothing but a worthless pimp. Your woman does all the work and then you come around and do all the collecting. Couldn't you folks just be honest about what you're doing and announce the price up front?"

Before Ramón could protest, Fargo rose, gun aimed at the man's sweat-soaked forehead. "You're going to drop that gun and sit on the bed with her until I'm out of here. Since it's too late to travel on tonight, I'm going to put on my duds and go find another room."

"But *señor*, you have shamed me, and I am a man of reputation," Ramón sputtered.

"Nobody will hear about this from me," Fargo promised.

Ramón slowly eased his gun back into its tooled-leather holster. "*Señor*, I ride here with my men, who are around here even now."

"You mean if I walk out of here all in one piece, they'll decide that you're a coward and you'll lose your standing? Or else they'll decide that you're hurt, and they owe you some vengeance, so they'll take it out on me?"

Ramón nodded. "That is the situation, *senõr*. If you were to leave quietly some way, I could fire my pistol into this thick wall—then they would think all was in order."

"I think you're full of shit," Fargo proclaimed as he used his pistol to motion Ramón over to the bed, where María Teresa still sat in silence, tugging a blanket over her bosom even though she had nothing to hide from either man.

The Trailsman swapped his pistol from hand to hand as he tugged on his shirt. "You're bluffing Ramón, and I'm calling your bluff. Your men are so busy getting drunk right now that they don't give a damn what happens to you."

Ramón slumped, his arm across María Teresa's shoulders, as Fargo finished dressing and stomped out of the room.

Fargo had been right about Ramón's men. There were four of them, all dressed pretty much like their boss, although their clothes weren't quite so neat. They sat at a wooden table in the dining room, which turned into a saloon after supper. They passed around a bottle of mescal. From the sound of their Spanish, they were bragging a lot about various women they had known. Two of them, though, had notably fair complexions, and they had to think a bit before they added their boasts to the conversation.

At the next table were three men, passing around a jug of corn liquor, and bragging in slurred English. At the other table sat one man alone, nursing a stiff shot of bourbon. Gray-bearded and shaggy, he was slim and limber, although he was getting up there in years. He was trying to look more relaxed than he really was. Fargo knew him.

It wasn't polite to hail men like that by name, however, because they may have changed names recently. So Fargo stepped closer and started with a question. "Can you tell me where to find Sanderson? I need to see him about a room and a bottle."

The man grunted before he looked up and recognized the Trailsman. "He'll be back shortly. Have a seat."

Fargo took the offer. "Mind if I call you Zeb?"

"Do as good as any, I suppose. You're still Skye Fargo?" He grinned, but there was no way the man could look happy with all those scars on his lined face.

The Trailsman nodded. "Yep. Just on my way from nowhere to no place, and thought I'd stop in here."

"Wondered where you came from. Didn't see you on the stage with them." He waved toward the three men with the corn liquor. Then he shook his head toward the mescal table. "And you didn't ride in with them either."

Zeb Reynolds had been a free trapper in Taos long ago, back when there was a market for beaver pelts and Bent's Old Fort was a going concern. When that had petered out, he'd started doing pretty much what the Trailsman did. Despite his age, Zeb was one of the better wagon masters, and still good at finding trails, blazing routes, and the like.

"How's the stage these days?" Fargo teased. "Never thought you'd get so old that you'd rather ride the stage than your own good horse."

Reynolds turned and spat before answering. "Bah. Ain't that old. Just simpler this way to get to my next job."

"They haven't put you out to pasture yet?" Fargo asked.

"Shit, no. Got me a good job with Uncle Sam. When the stage pulls out for the Pueblo tomorrow, I'll be aboard. And when I get there, I'll go on the payroll."

He suddenly became quiet as Ramón entered the room. Ramón's eyes flashed at Fargo. The Trailsman's hand started for his gun, but then Ramón's mouth turned up a bit. His expression seemed to be asking whether Fargo had told anybody about their recent encounter in María Teresa's room. Fargo shook his head slightly. Ramón slowly nodded, looking more pleasant by the second, and went over to join his men.

Right on his heels was the station agent, Jared Sanderson, who wore muttonchop whiskers so long that they brushed his shoulders. Fargo called for a bottle of bourbon and told Sanderson he'd be needing a room. Sanderson winked and muttered something under his breath about how María Teresa ought to be horsewhipped. Then he explained that he was booked solid for the night.

Zeb told Fargo he was welcome to his floor, then began bragging at length about his new job. The government was starting an official survey of the mountainous parts of the West. The survey crew had been working down around Santa Fe. After finishing there, they would move north.

Surveyors made maps, but when they started the job, they didn't necessarily know a whole lot about the territory. To keep from getting themselves lost, they hired guides who knew a given area.

"So, for three dollars a day, plus bacon and beans and my very own government mule, I'll lead them fancy-pants surveyors around the mountains," Zeb boasted. "We'll go up the Arkansas a spell from the Pueblo, where I'm supposed to meet up with 'em this week. Then up the Hardscrabble, over to the Greenhorn, across the Sangres—"

"The old Taos Trapper's Trail," Fargo interjected. "Hell, a blind man wouldn't need a guide for that."

"I'm not just showing the way," Zeb continued. "You do some hunting for fresh meat, help tend the stock, and cook some. They bring a couple of their own strikers to help, but you still do a considerable amount of the chores, so that they have time in the evening to draw their maps and write down what they saw and did that day.

"It's not all that adventurous, like the old days," Zeb admitted. Seeming inclined to lapse into embroidered tales of bygone times, Zeb paused before casting a wistful smile toward Fargo. "But it's easy work at top pay," he concluded.

In the past, Zeb had enjoyed a reputation for taking audacious risks. For those who knew him, Zeb Reynolds' youthful exploits made better lore than the tales about Jim Beckwourth or Old Bill Williams. The old-timer's braggadocio concerning his new job struck Fargo as sad.

"There're worse ways to spend a summer," Fargo agreed after swallowing two fingers' worth of wretched bourbon and passing the bottle to Zeb.

Zeb matched Fargo's swig and belched. "Indeed there are. And it's tolerable safe work, too. Redskins don't pester surveyors much, and the folks that're settled love to see the surveyors."

Most folks in the West didn't like to see anybody from the government, so Fargo asked why surveyors were an exception.

"I'm not a lawyer, so I can't tell you all of it. But the way I understand it, if you go off and squat somewhere and start raisin' corn or cows or whatever, you can't get a legal title to the land you're on till it's been surveyed. Then the government has a proper description of where your land ends and another man's starts. Most folks like the idea of owning their land, fair and square, so the surveyors get a decent welcome."

The rest of the room must have been interested in government surveys, because as Zeb continued after pulling down some more bourbon, the other chatter had stopped and everybody was watching him. He obviously enjoyed having a bigger audience.

" 'Course, when I guided Lieutenant John Gunnison and his boys through the Sangres and over into the San Luis Valley back in '53, they were lookin' for a railroad route with easy grades, water stops, and coal outcrops. Fancy that, a railroad across that fearsome country. It'll never happen. You know how the government likes to waste money. Shit, they had an artist to draw pictures, and an astronomer that stared at the stars ever' night, and this quack German surgeon that couldn't set a bone or dig out a bullet, though he talked a mighty fine spiel."

Although the Trailsman had never guided a survey, he had a fair idea of what was involved. But if he was going to spread his bedroll on the floor of Zeb's room, he'd better stay on the good side of the old bullshitter. Fargo sipped at the bottle and continued to humor Zeb by acting a lot more interested than he really was. The truth was, the old man's early exploits made for a lot better listening than his current work, but Zeb's pride seemed to demand that he prove his continuing worth.

"Now this survey that's comin' up is different," Zeb proceeded. "It's not for some railroad that'll never be built. They're doin' something half useful, figuring out some boundary lines."

"Boundaries?" The question came from one of the blond-haired men at the mescal table. His accent was harsh and guttural, not like the melodious inflections that the others spoke.

"What I hear is that they're gonna settle, once and for all, just where some of the old Mexican land grants begin and end. That oughtta please a lot of folks."

Ramón, who was at that same table, didn't look a bit pleased. "Which land grant, *señor*?"

"There's a passel of 'em over in the San Luis Valley—Baca Grant, Beaubien and Miranda, Conejos, Medano and Zapato, Sangre de Cristo—hell maybe some more. Those are just the ones I recollect. Like it or not, they're going to set corners on all of 'em."

"Would one be the Espinoza Grant?" Surprisingly, the question did not come from Ramón, but from the man at his side, a lean, fair-haired man with hard, chiseled features and bright-blue eyes that were starting to glow in the lamplight. He looked German, or perhaps Dutch or Swedish, and he spoke in guttural tones.

Zeb shrugged. "Could be." He pulled at the whiskey. "What those surveyor boys work on is up to them, not me. I'm just a hired man." He turned back to face Fargo.

But the old trapper was interrupted by another question from the flaxen-haired man. "What would happen if they did not have your services, sir?"

Zeb Reynolds should have kept his mouth shut, but he obviously enjoyed the chance to brag about just how important he would be.

"Without me, without a guide, why, hell, those surveyors couldn't do any work at all. If I didn't show up to meet 'em, then they'd just have to pack it in for the year."

"Indeed. So the survey would be delayed if you were not to appear at the Pueblo at the proper time."

The old trapper gave a broad grin that showed just how many teeth he was missing. "You got it, friend." He wiped his mouth with a greasy fringed buckskin sleeve and reached for the bottle.

His talonlike hand never quite grasped the whiskey. The sudden and unexpected bullet caught him just inside his armpit, spinning him off his chair as he tumbled back against the wall. Fargo's ears rang from the deafening report of a pistol fired at close range. The Trailsman sprang to Zeb's side. On his way, he kicked their table over, giving them some cover at the cost of the spilled whiskey.

In the haze of swirling, acrid, powder smoke, Fargo saw that the three men at the closer table had the same idea. But the bullet had come from Ramón's table, likely from the fair-haired man who was hurrying out the door with the others.

Fargo's Colt was out in an instant, but that wasn't soon enough. His round just pushed into the door frame, a hairbreadth behind the brim of the last fleeing man's hat.

He began to rise to pursue them, but Zeb's awful moan pulled him back to the old trapper's side.

Zeb's visage now looked gray and drawn, as if something behind him were pulling the flesh back and stretching it across the bones of his face. His teeth were clenched and he fought for each breath. The pool of blood by his shoulder spread across the buckskin shirt.

"They hulled me good," he whispered. "I'm a goner."

"Bullshit," Fargo grunted. With his belt knife, he opened Zeb's pullover buckskin shirt and found the wound, about midway between the trapper's right armpit and the closest nipple. A little lower, and the shot would have definitely ruined a lung. But that wasn't the case, because Zeb wasn't coughing up any frothy blood. Even so, the shot must have shattered at least one rib, because a bone had stopped the bullet. There wasn't any exit wound.

Wishing there was a regular doctor at hand to tend to this, Fargo hollered at the three men. Just two yards away, they were still crouched against the wall, with the tipped table before them. "Get some clean rags and hot water from the kitchen," he ordered. They remained in place, quivering and staring. "Now," he demanded, and one finally rose and scurried off.

"Not bleedin' much, is it?" Zeb wondered, his voice hoarse and labored.

"Just stay still and keep your damn mouth shut, and you'll do fine," Fargo consoled as the rags arrived, along with a bowl of steaming water.

Zeb flinched as Fargo swabbed the torn flesh. He muttered a few protests, and before a preoccupied Fargo could stop him, he tried to sit up. That motion twisted the sharp ends of a shattered bone inside his chest. A gusher of crimson from a fresh-torn artery spouted into the Trailsman's eyes. He planted a fist in the old trapper's jaw, knocking him cold, but it still took a few minutes to get the wound packed enough to stanch the flow. By now the ashen-faced Zeb certainly did look like a goner.

2

"Dammit, Fargo, couldn't you find a better way than this? What the hell are you doing up there? You takin' me hostage or somethin'?"

It was one of Zeb's first coherent statements since he'd been shot four days ago. The Trailsman didn't see much up ahead except dust and sagebrush, so he decided it was safe to turn from the driver's seat of this creaking, high-railed Studebaker farm wagon.

Right behind the lumbering wagon, the Ovaro walked comfortably. Not so comfortable, perhaps, was Zeb. With his arms flailing and grasping at the rails for support, the old trapper tried to sit up from the cornhusk-stuffed mattress that the Trailsman had lashed over a load of vegetables.

"Lie back down, Zeb, or I'll tie you down." Fargo kept his tone light, almost bantering, but his dust-streaked face showed he was serious.

Zeb eased back, but he couldn't stay quiet. His questions were easily heard over the purl of iron tires rolling through the dust, the jingle of the harness on the two mottled gray percherons ahead, and the steady, slow rhythm of their huge plodding hooves.

"What the hell am I doing here, atop a load of goddamn cucumbers?" Zeb rasped.

"It's not a load of cucumbers," Fargo explained. "It's summer squash. Seems that Mrs. Sanderson's garden exceeded all expectations this summer."

Zeb took a minute to digest that and decided he couldn't. "Fargo, you mind tellin' me where I am and just where we're bound?"

"We just forded Chico Creek, or to be precise, the gulch where Chico Creek sometimes runs. So we're maybe five miles east of the Pueblo, which is where we're headed. You really ought to know, since it was your idea to get to the Pueblo."

Zeb grunted and ground his teeth. He was hurting more than he let on. "Well, I was bound for the Pueblo to meet up with the government surveyors before I got myself shot. Gave 'em my word on it. So I'm damn happy that that's where we're bound, but I don't remember it being my idea to get there by laying on my back atop a load of goddamn cucumbers."

"Squash," Fargo corrected before exhaling slowly. "Indeed, you did get yourself shot, Zeb. And you made it worse than it needed to be, the way you twisted around afterward. You damn near bled to death. Next morning, you came around some, though maybe you don't remember that."

Zeb muttered something that sounded like agreement. Before continuing, Fargo scanned the countryside. A quarter-mile to his left, the cottonwoods that lined the Arkansas provided the only greenery in sight. To his right and to the rear spread rolling, summer-browned prairie, spotted with gray-green clumps of yucca and sage. Up ahead, the Rocky Mountains reared up, stretching from the remote twin pyramids of the Spanish Peaks to the looming blue cone of Pikes Peak.

"Come the next morning," the Trailsman recounted, "you were moaning about how you had to get to the Pueblo, with or without my help. I told you I was your friend and I wouldn't let you bleed to death, which you surely would have done had you tried to get there on your own."

"Gave my word," Zeb grumped. "And besides, I was planning to ride that stagecoach, which may sway a lot, but it doesn't shake enough to start me bleedin' again."

"Zeb, I asked some questions. Fact is, the Kansas City, Santa Fe & Canon City Fast Line uses regular Concord coaches on their main run between Kansas City and Santa Fe. For their side run, up the Arkansas from Bent's Fort to Canon City, however, they save a few nickels. They use regular old spine-jarring wagons, and they drive them hard and fast. You'd have been drowning in your own blood before you got two miles. But since you were so damn determined to get to the Pueblo, and since Mrs. Sanderson, the stage agent's wife, wanted to ship some of her summer squash up to the company's eating house at the Pueblo, well, it all worked out. I'm getting you there, slowly and easily. Maybe so slowly that you'll be healed up some by the time we get there."

As the produce wagon topped a rise, Fargo was rewarded with a view of the Pueblo. It was less than an hour away, even when you considered fording Fountain Creek. Although it was a hundred yards wide, the meandering creek seldom ran more than a foot deep. You could cross it anywhere, if you didn't mind quicksand. This ford, at the top of a tree-lined oxbow, was about as solid as any.

The horses slowed almost to a halt as they approached the water. Zeb, curious about what was around him, sat up and stuck his head over the rails.

"Dammit, Zeb, lay your head back down and hold still while we cross the creek," Fargo ordered. He urged the horses on, though they seemed a bit reluctant. Was it the usual contrary and lazy nature of horseflesh, or had they sensed something he hadn't?

Quiet. That's what it was. The trees alongside any prairie water were always loud with the chatter of magpies, but this morning there were no raucous cries from the greenery.

That meant something unusual had scared the birds away from the ford, only a couple hundred yards ahead. Fargo checked to make sure his pistol was at hand, then leaned over and pulled his Sharps carbine out of its canvas scabbard.

Bending down may have saved his life. As he started to straighten, a bullet whistled over him, just where his head would have been. Fargo heard the thunderous report of a long-barreled Sharps fired from a hundred yards away. Clutching the reins, he jerked the draft horses to a halt and lay prone on the footboard while he looked for the telltale puff of smoke.

It came from a dense clump of chokecherry bushes. Although it was out of pistol range, Fargo sent a shot that way before working his Sharps up to where he could shoulder it. "Who's shooting at us?" Zeb wondered from the back.

"I don't know," Fargo grunted. "But keep yourself down. I can handle this."

The Trailsman got his Sharps shouldered. As he squeezed a bullet toward the bushes, another gun sounded. It wasn't Zeb, since he didn't have one handy back there, and besides, it came from the other side of the wagon.

Fargo frowned. They were out in the open, and caught in a crossfire between two hidden bushwhackers. If robbers had set up shop at this ford, they were certainly going through a lot of trouble to get a load of squash.

Fargo saw some movement in the bush before him and made sure that at least one ambusher would pay with his life. Undeterred by twigs and leaves, the heavy Sharps bullet plowed straight to the unseen attacker. It thudded into flesh. Although his ears were ringing with the report of his own gun, Fargo heard some thrashing, followed by the dull collapse of a body.

There was no way to be sure that this man was out of action permanently, but it was certain that the one on the other side was still up to no good. The trick was to get turned around without exposing himself, and Fargo's cover wasn't any wider than a coffin.

The wagon jostled, and Fargo told Zeb again to stay put. The old trapper insisted on trying to sit up, however, which brought his hat above the side rails. That drew a shot from the downstream ambusher, who would now need a couple seconds to reload.

Moving with the speed and smoothness of a cat, Fargo used the time to turn around. His action provoked a hurried shot from behind a downed cottonwood log. The whizzing bullet missed him by better than a yard.

With a jerk that rolled Fargo back, the wagon jumped forward and picked up speed. As the horses raced toward the water, Fargo reached for the reins, but they weren't where he thought they should be. Actually, they weren't anywhere that his waving right hand could reach.

"Hold on, Zeb," Fargo shouted as the old man stuck up his head, hoping to get some idea of what was happening.

The rising hat didn't attract any bullets. Way out of his reach, the reins were trailing in Fountain Creek. The ribbons must have tumbled forward when the horses started running, which was forgivable, given the nasty and bleeding crease on the near percheron's dappled rump. Fargo couldn't blame that horse for wanting to get somewhere else in a hurry, and its partner in the harness didn't have any choice but to go along.

Out of control and pulled by two strong and frightened horses, the produce wagon rolled smoothly across the sandy bottom, then hit dry land with a savage bounce that nearly tossed Fargo from his swaying perch.

With his hand clutching the seat, Fargo got to his knees. He was facing backward and couldn't see much of Zeb except the mattress. He turned and muttered something soothing to the horses, but if they heard him, they didn't pay any attention. As Fargo turned, another bullet came from the rear, just missing Zeb as it smacked into the load and turned half a dozen green squash into a spraying fountain of instant relish.

The noise inspired the horses to pick up their hurried gait. If this kept up, Zeb was going to get bounced around, or maybe even out, and that wouldn't do him any good. A line of fresh blood already showed at the shoulder of Zeb's flannel shirt.

The only way to settle the horses was to leap from the footboard, land on a horse's back, and grab the reins. But when Fargo turned and began to stand for the leap, the wagon hit a rut. The laden wagon stayed intact, but the jolt sent Fargo upward, into the sights of the ambusher, who had now stepped out for a better view.

Up just long enough to get a look at the man, Fargo came back down before his bullet arrived. From this distance, more than two hundred yards, the lean man who was shooting looked an awful lot like the blond man who'd shot Zeb back at Bent's Old Fort.

Fargo thought about returning fire, but decided against it. The wagon was bounding so much that he didn't have a shot—not from this range, anyway. Standing up would be the only way to get a shot, and staying aboard would mean grasping a rail, which took a hand he'd need for using his Sharps. If there had been any cover, Fargo might have jumped off.

But the wagon was climbing quickly out of the valley anyway, so they'd soon be out of range, and out of sight, of the man back there. So the best thing was to keep Zeb from getting hurt.

Reluctantly, Fargo shoved his Sharps into the load of shifting squash and crawled toward Zeb. The old trapper had rolled to one side. Both his talonlike hands had a white-knuckled grip on the rail. When the wagon crested the rise, however, the left wheel slammed against a protruding stone with such rocking force that Zeb was tossed to the other side of the wagon.

Much more of this, and Zeb wouldn't have a chance.

Fargo crawled over the squash to where Zeb was, and found his hand reaching into warm blood.

Shit. The wound had come open with all this thrashing and churning. Maybe he could keep Zeb from moving much more until the horses finally settled down. Now that they weren't getting shot at anymore, there was a chance of restoring some order.

For perhaps a minute, the frightened horses continued to gallop forward. Lying prone, Fargo steadied himself, by pushing his right hand and his boot against the rail. He got his other arm across Zeb, pinning him down on part of the cornhusk mattress. "Just take it easy, old-timer," he whispered. "Things will settle down here shortly."

The heaving, lathered horses finally plodded to a halt and Fargo rolled forward to set the brake. He scanned the countryside warily before stepping out and returning with the reins, which he tied to the brake handle. Nothing out there looked dangerous, and they were close enough to the Pueblo so that shots might attract attention, which was the last thing most bushwhackers wanted.

Now it was time to tend to Zeb, who lay ashen-faced as his spreading red blood seeped into the bright-green vegetables and the pale cotton cover of the mattress. His eyes were blinking and he was still breathing, so Fargo figured there was a chance.

Zeb didn't. "Waugh," he spat, his voice hoarse and labored. "I'm a gone coon, that's what I am."

"Bullshit," Fargo countered, but he found himself agreeing when Zeb didn't reply right away. Instead, he coughed, and frothy blood bubbled out of his lips and spread across his gray-white mustache.

"You'll tell them government boys I tried, won't you?" Zeb rasped as his eyelids fluttered.

"Better than that, I'll get you there," Fargo soothed, although he doubted that Zeb would arrive alive. When a man bled on the outside, you could usually do something to keep his life from flowing away. Coughing up blood meant a man was bleeding on the inside, however, and there wasn't much the Trailsman, or anybody, could do about that.

Nonetheless, Fargo tried. After repacking the shoulder wound, he shifted things to make Zeb comfortable. Maybe they could manage the last mile to the Pueblo, where there might be a doctor who could handle things from there.

Fargo poured a trickle of water over Zeb's pale lips. The old trapper finally opened them, so that he could quench his burning thirst. Then he spoke.

"Fargo, it's no use. Don't try anymore. You've done all you could. Even if I was to pull through . . ." It took him six tries to catch his breath, and he didn't have much voice despite all that work. "I'd be too banged up to do anything. Better off dead than that."

Fargo grasped the trapper's cold hand and wiped his feverish brow with a bandanna. "You'll do fine. Just let me get us into the Pueblo."

He shook his head against the spasms that made his body quiver. "No, Fargo. I got a few minutes left of this life, and I don't want to waste 'em. Now hear me."

In truth, that was about all that Fargo could do for the dying man, although he hated to give up. He grudgingly settled into the squash and continued to mop Zeb's face with the wet bandanna while using his other hand to hold Zeb's hat to keep the glaring sun out of his lined face.

"You'll see the surveyors, won't you?"

"I will," Fargo promised. "I'll tell them that you did your damnedest to get there on time."

"Good." Zeb already looked more comfortable, although less lively. "Now that I'm cashing in, what's mine is yours, Fargo. Ain't got much, but you might come up with a pile of gold if you can find that map in my possibles."

"Map?"

"It's parchment, all folded up in some wadding. It's a treasure map, Fargo."

This wasn't the time to argue, though Fargo knew that he'd be a wealthy man by now if he had just a nickel for every bullshit treasure tale he'd ever heard.

Always there were Spanish conquistadors who had discovered some fabulous lode a century or two ago. As the stories generally went, they enslaved a few local Indians to do all the hard work of mining, then killed the Indians and started back to Mexico with their booty.

"How'd you come by it?" Might as well humor a dying man.

Zeb's breaths were coming easier now, but they were shallow, so shallow that he couldn't reply for a bit. Fargo thought of the other treasure tales. On the way back to Mexico, the conquistadors got attacked by Indians, or they got stuck in some desert, or maybe a blizzard forced them to halt. Anyway, they cached their fortune. Only one survived, of course, and he never could get back to recover the hidden wealth—but there was always a map that got passed along. Some folks were even dumb enough to buy such maps.

"Long story, Fargo," Zeb whispered. "The map came from an hidalgo lady in Taos who got killed in the uprising back in '47. We were married, more or less. Maybe you can make somethin' of it, for I never could."

"Any more to the story?" Fargo wondered as he felt Zeb's gnarled hand grow cold and colder.

"Just the usual," Zeb conceded, the words coming at irregular intervals. "Spanish soldiers and a priest, lookin' around to the north. Priest was the only one to get back. He made up the map, gave it to his bishop, who gave it to a nephew, who was my woman's granddad. She's gone. . . ."

With that, the old trapper rattled his last breath and took off to join her.

Fargo slowly closed Zeb's eyes. Through all the

bouncing today, Zeb's saddlebags still sat near the tailgate of the wagon, so Fargo grabbed the leather pouches before returning to the driver's seat.

Before looking for Zeb's map, he again scanned the countryside and saw nothing that looked dangerous. Just a sleepy town up ahead, where everyone except the buzzing flies was sensibly avoiding the heat of day by indulging in a noontime siesta.

The flies were busy, though, swarming around the open gash on the near horse's rump. Fargo pulled some salve out of his saddlebag to tend to that. While he soothed the percheron, his own Ovaro arrived; the big pinto stallion had sensibly taken cover somewhere during the gunplay. Fargo started the team toward the Pueblo and mulled over this morning's events.

Back at Bent's Old Fort, Zeb had been shot by a knife-thin, fair-haired man who didn't fit in at a table of swarthy Mexicans. He was probably the same man who'd done most of the shooting during the attempted ambush at the ford.

Men picked up enemies. Fargo knew that, but Zeb didn't seem to have known that man. So why would he shoot there? And then try again here?

Fargo concentrated on the first shooting. Though there had been a cuckolded husband at that table who might have been angry enough to draw on the Trailsman, Ramón had not been the one to shoot. It was that fair-haired man. And he hadn't started shooting until Zeb had boasted some about how the surveyors couldn't function without him as their guide.

"You'd get the idea that somebody doesn't want this survey to happen," Fargo muttered to himself as they reached the irrigated gardens at the edge of the Pueblo. "After Zeb's brag, a man might think that stopping Zeb would stop the survey. Then, when that didn't work, they set up at the ford across Fountain Creek, which you pretty well have to cross if you're going from Bent's Old Fort to the Pueblo. That stands to reason, because they didn't start firing at us until

Zeb stuck his fool head up, which ended up with him getting killed, though they never hit anything except a horse's rump."

So somebody who was connected to Ramón seemed intent on stopping the government's survey. Where had they been planning to survey? Weren't they going to establish boundaries for old Spanish land grants over in the San Luis Valley? Zeb had mentioned that most grant holders welcomed the mapmakers, because it meant that their claims to vast stretches of land were official and accepted by the United States and its territorial governments.

So why would these men be so opposed to a survey that they'd take up murder and ambush? Maybe there would be an answer back at the ford, if the ambusher Fargo had shot was indeed dead and if the body was still there. Sometimes men carried things in their pockets that would tell you what you wanted to know. But if the body remained there now, it would probably still be there tomorrow, and Fargo had chores to tend to in the Pueblo.

The Pueblo wasn't really a pueblo. Not the way folks generally thought of a pueblo, with huge adobe buildings like those down in New Mexico Territory that whole tribes lived in, each family with a room or two.

Up here, the Pueblo had started out as a ramshackle adobe fortress where Fountain Creek joined the Arkansas. It had been one of the roughest places in the West, because in its early days, the Arkansas River formed the boundary between the United States and Mexico. Men wanted by the law on either side of the border found it a convenient place to hole up. The Pueblo attracted trappers whose characters were so low that no one would abide by them, along with traders who sold whiskey and guns to the Indians. They were among the more respectable elements there.

Fargo had never seen it, because on Christmas Day, 1854, about fifty surly Utes found their way inside the fortress and butchered everyone they could find. The slaughter of fourteen people—two boys and a woman had been taken captive—became a legend. The Pueblo, though, had been abandoned that instant, and a spring flood several years later had swept it away so that even its foundations were hidden.

The new settlement, which had sprung up with the gold rush of 1859, looked even less like a pueblo. It was just another overnight supply town for the mining camps in the mountains to the west. It boasted a few adobes, but most of the buildings were ramshackle wood structures with false fronts. But the place was still called "the Pueblo," even though the name didn't fit at all.

Its sunbaked, dusty main street boasted two hotels, several stores that sold everything from ladies' notions to miners' tools, a greengrocer's shop, and at last, the livery stable, which was across the street from the stage depot, where Fargo had promised to deliver this load of summer squash. That is, if they still wanted it, what with the blood back there and the corpse atop the load.

Before he could pull up properly, a heavy-set, dark man came running out. "You would be Signor Fargo?" he inquired, his arms waving with every word. At first, Fargo thought the accent was Spanish, but he decided that wasn't right—the man was Italian.

The Trailsman nodded. "I am."

"Signor Sanderson sent word you would be coming with a wagon of the zuccheto squash. It is certainly welcome, for a late frost this spring ruined our planting."

"There's more than that," Fargo cautioned before the man could step around and look inside the wagon. "We ran into some trouble."

"Trouble? Do tell me all about it, for it is also my honor to serve as the constable of the Pueblo, Signor Fargo." He pulled a polished seven-pointed star out of his shirt pocket, just in case Fargo doubted his word.

The Trailsman braked the wagon and stepped down. His host shook hands and introduced himself as Guido

Marcantoni, and it was fine to call him Guido. The Trailsman explained the body in the back by recounting the shootings at Bent's Old Fort and the Fountain ford.

"This is all most confusing to me, Signor Fargo," Guido protested as they stepped inside the stage depot for something to drink.

"Can't say it's all real straight in my mind, either," Fargo agreed. "But I'm sure there's a reason somewhere."

"I hope so." Guido snapped his fingers.

Even if she was a bit on the plump side, the girl who emerged from the door to the kitchen still looked voluptuous. But Fargo told himself to ignore such thoughts, since it was obvious, from the way she tried to shrug off serving them some wine, that she was Guido's daughter.

"You see, Signor Fargo," Guido continued as the cool red wine arrived, "a stranger rode through our town not an hour ago, with a body on his horse. He was fair and lean, like the man you talk about. He told me his friend had an accident while hunting along the river, so we let him ride on."

Fargo shrugged. "Suppose that made sense, given what you knew then."

"But now it is most perplexing, *signor*, for your story is very different from his. Perhaps you would not mind staying in town a few days until we can find this other man and determine what really happened?"

Fargo minded like hell. He wanted to stay only long enough to turn Zeb's body over to the undertaker, and to keep his promise to tell the surveyors that Zeb had lost his life in his effort to keep his word.

Guido was just trying to do his bounden duty as constable, and he was being polite about it, asking Fargo to stay around instead of tossing him in jail. Every time Guido's luscious daughter came within sight, however, Fargo felt a stirring that could lead to nothing but more trouble if he stayed around the Pueblo.

Was there any quick and easy way to get out of town without offending or shooting Guido?

"I don't have any problem with that," Fargo conceded with another shrug and a sip of the sweet red wine. "But the federal government might get a bit bothered if its surveyors are delayed on your account. The last I heard, they're planning to leave any minute, as soon as their guide gets here. And I'm going to be their guide. You wouldn't want to make the army and the federal marshals angry, would you, Guido?"

3

"I've heard of you, Skye Fargo." Captain Josiah Macomber, who looked too young to be an officer and too dapper to be anything else, twirled one end of his steerhorn mustache into a sharp point. With his right hand, he grabbed another glass of Taos Lightning, the only whiskey to be found in the Pueblo on this steaming summer afternoon.

"Hope you don't hold what you've heard against me." The Trailsman shifted, trying to get comfortable in the squeaking wooden chair, and decided it was impossible. At least it was in the right place, so he could keep his back to the adobe wall and see whoever might enter through the thick plank door.

Macomber laughed. "Most of it was good. Quite good, as a matter of fact. You wouldn't be known as the Trailsman unless you were among the best at leading parties through wilderness."

"Where you're headed is hardly wilderness," Fargo reminded. "It might have been when Fremont came through in the winter of '48 when the Great Pathfinder managed to get himself lost. But by '54, when Gunnison passed by, there were a couple of towns. Now settlements and farms are popping up all over the San Luis Valley, raising crops to sell to the miners. Besides, trappers and traders have been going through here since about a week after time began."

The round-faced captain, his dark hair close-cropped,

nodded in agreement. "Be that as it may, it's new country to me. We need a guide, and I'm grateful that you've offered your services after tragedy struck Zeb Reynolds."

Fargo flexed his arms and hoped that the potent, throat-burning whiskey would soothe the cramps he felt developing from this flimsy chair. Fargo hadn't quite offered his services to Captain Macomber's survey party. Zeb's last request had been for Fargo to explain how hard Zeb had tried to keep his word, and that was mostly why the Trailsman had found Macomber at a camp on the edge of the Pueblo.

But there was more. Somebody had been shooting at them, and among the things that Fargo disliked, getting shot at ranked high on the list. The only reason that made any sense was that the attempts on Zeb's life had something to do with this survey. Fargo wanted some answers, and hiring on as their guide looked like the best way to get those answers. It was also the easiest way to get out of this town when the town fathers were understandably curious about the bodies that kept showing up around the Trailsman.

"As I understand it, I'll get five dollars a day." Fargo raised his lake-blue eyes to halt the flickering of Macomber's brown eyes. The captain had been sitting still, but his face betrayed his haste to get a guide hired and get on with his work.

"The going rate for guides is three dollars a day, but we'll pay you five," Macomber agreed. "I'm sure you can get us where we need to go, which is the main part of your work."

"What are the other parts? I've guided pack trains, wagon trains, and army troops, but I've never worked with a survey crew."

"It will be a lot like those other jobs," Macomber explained. "You'll be in charge of finding campsites and getting everybody from one to the next, that sort of thing. But I have to warn you that you may not find a survey party easy to work with."

"How's that?"

Macomber sighed. "In a way, you and the people under you—the strikers and packers, the cook, and the wrangler—you end up being servants, of a sort. It's your job to take care of all the tedious chores, all the grunt work, so that the surveyors can concentrate on doing their work, which they think is the only important thing in the world. There'll be times you'll think that you're working with a bunch of spoiled children."

"Hadn't thought of that," Fargo granted. "But you're in charge, aren't you? Isn't this a military operation?"

"Not exactly." Macomber worked on the other point of his waxed mustache. "It's actually run by the Interior Department, not the War Department. This isn't a military survey. We're not looking for places to put forts or to find routes for new roads. We're out here to produce accurate maps of the local routes that people already use, so that those who come in the future will know the way. The major goal, though, is to finally establish the boundaries of several Mexican land grants."

"So why is an army captain in charge?"

"Experience. I've done this before, and from what I heard, the Interior Department couldn't find any civilians who'd run surveys in the West. We started last May, down in New Mexico Territory. Now that the snowpacks have melted from the mountains up here, we'll spend about six weeks in the field and then head back to Fort Leavenworth to put everything together."

That made sense. "So what happens now?"

"Much of that is up to you, Fargo. The schedule isn't real rigid. We'll outfit here at the Pueblo. You'll need to consult with our quartermaster, Sergeant O'Reilly, about what supplies to buy. You'll need to hire a wrangler and assemble a string of pack mules. We have about a dozen we brought up from New Mexico, but we will need more once we're off the beaten path. It usually works best if the wrangler hires his own packers, but that's up to you. You'll also need to hire a cook. I'd like it if we were ready to go within a week."

This was starting to sound like a bigger job than Fargo had envisioned. "Outside of the crew I put on, how many people are we talking about here?"

"Let me see. There's O'Reilly and myself. We have a surgeon, Doctor Krantz, who's also our astronomer."

"Astronomer? I thought you were mapping the ground, not the sky."

"The way to establish your position on the earth is to look to the heavens. You establish due north by sighting Polaris, and you derive your latitude from its angular elevation—"

"I get the idea," Fargo interrupted.

"We have a cartographer, William Gibson."

"He's drawn some pretty maps," Fargo conceded, "though they're a bit on the fanciful side—that man ought to bill himself as an artist, not a mapmaker. Last map I saw of his had the Arkansas headwatering up by the Snake, and the Rio Grande wandering around by the Great Salt Lake, near the head of the Buenaventura River, which doesn't exist."

"This time his maps will be correct." Macomber's steely tone indicated that he had discussed this at considerable and forceful length with Gibson. "Edmund Wilkes, the famous landscape artist, will also be accompanying us."

"You did say this was a survey party, didn't you?"

Macomber looked taken aback. "Of course. Why do you ask?"

"Because you haven't mentioned any surveyors yet."

"Oh." His mustache started to twitch as four men, all dusty and dressed like cattle drovers, walked behind him, to get from the front door to the bar. His eyes mere slits, Fargo watched them closely, but the men, after casting cursory glances their way, looked more interested in getting the bartender's attention.

"We'll have two surveyors. They're due in any day."

At Fargo's nod, Macomber continued after refilling his shotglass. "Each surveyor has two chainmen, two axmen, and a compassman."

"So the pair of surveyors account for a dozen people. With your artist and your mapmaker, your surgeon, you, and your quartermaster, we'll have seventeen men there. Then a wrangler, some help for him, a cook . . . Looks like I'd better plan on about two dozen men in the party, and you want to be ready to head out in a week."

The young captain nodded. "Keep in mind that we'll have a lot of gear with our tents and instruments."

At least two pack mules per man, plus a mount or two apiece, Fargo decided. That would be about seventy-five animals to keep track of. A good packer could get a mule ready to go in about ten minutes. You didn't want to spend all day just getting ready to go, so they'd need at least six packers, who could also help with the other camp chores—cutting firewood, digging latrines, gathering meat, picketing the stock, and standing night guard if that became necessary.

One of the four men standing at the bar snapped his head back to face the mirror at the rear when Fargo lifted his eyes after finishing his thought. The man had been eavesdropping and was trying to pretend that he hadn't been. Was the bowlegged man with the chest-length dark beard just trying to cover up his bad manners?

Fargo kept his eyes on the man while explaining to Macomber that they should be able to hire most of the help for the usual dollar-a-day. The cook and the wrangler would get at least double that. Talking money could be difficult, but it was best to get this settled now, so that there wouldn't be any surprises or arguments later.

All that sounded reasonable to the captain, whose only caution was to bargain hard for mules. "When we outfitted in El Paso this spring, we were in too big a hurry and ended up paying twenty dollars a head. I hope you can do better than that."

Fargo nodded and examined the man standing at the bar again. This time the man was still looking forward, toward the mirror. It sported a pleasant reflection of the huge painting above Fargo's table: a comely, if somewhat plump, woman who was standing amid some trees. She had no clothes on, but her smooth hands were modestly crossed where her pale thighs came together. Much as the man might have been eyeballing the reflected painting, though, he had his left hand up by his ear, cupped so he could hear what was behind him. The only thing behind him was Fargo's conversation with Macomber about the survey.

Fargo's suspicions grew when the man at the bar muttered something to his neighbor and then started walking out. With every step, he made a visible effort not to look toward the Trailsman and the army captain.

As soon as the man eased himself out the plank door, Fargo leaned toward Macomber. "Don't let anybody else out the front door till you hear from me."

Macomber's pencil-thin eyebrows raised.

"Don't go out yourself, either." After cautioning the captain, Fargo rose and headed for the end of the bar, to a slot on the right side that led to the back door.

His purposeful steps were interrupted by a greeting from one of the men at the bar. "Heard you're lookin' for a wrangler, mister." The speaker was the man closest to Fargo. He was about as thin as full-grown men get, with sandy, shoulder-length hair and a three-day start on a beard. From the pinch-faced look of him, he'd come in too late for the daily free lunch.

"I might be in need of a wrangler, but at the moment, I'd like some answers," Fargo granted. His arm swung up and he grabbed the drover's dusty and patched wool shirt. "You want to tell me why your friend stepped outside? You know, the long-bearded guy that told you I might want to hire a wrangler?"

Fear, or maybe anger, flicked across the man's gray-green eyes. "He said he thought he might know where to find some mules to sell to you. He said he'd better hurry, so he would get to you first."

"Mighty nosy, aren't you? Snooping on other folks' talk that way? Now it's my turn to snoop a little. Who is he? Who are you?" Fargo tightened his grip on the man's shirt and made sure that the other two could hear his demanding tone.

"Lank. Lank Hobbs. That's what I go by. This here's Charlie Slater." His head twisted the other way. "He's Will Masters."

"Your friend that just stepped out?"

Lank looked perplexed. Will Masters helped him out. "He just said his name was Doakes. Luke Doakes, I think."

"You boys were drinking with him and didn't know him?"

Slater answered this time. "We met him on the street. He said he was looking for a man that matches the way you look, mister, along with an army captain. I told him I thought I'd seen you two step in here. Luke came in with us and liked what he saw enough to buy us all a drink. That man's got some pair of ears, I'll tell you. He told us what he heard you and the captain talking about."

"Why do you care?"

"Mister," Lank replied, "talk is that most of the mines in Colorado Territory have just about run out of gold. True or not, that makes things mighty slow, because folks quit comin' west, and a lot of them that're here decide to leave for better pickings, over to the Comstock or up to Montana."

"You haven't answered me yet," Fargo prodded.

Lank took a deep breath. "What that all means is that there isn't a lot of work here. And men like us that don't have jobs get mighty curious when they hear that there might be some work, even if it isn't quite polite just how they hear of it."

Fargo relaxed. These men weren't in on anything with Doakes. But what was Doakes up to?

"So Doakes was looking for me when you ran across him?"

Three nods replied.

"Guess I'll see what he's up to, then." Fargo released his grip on Lank's shirt and resumed his progress to the back door.

"But Doakes went out the front," Lank advised.

Fargo paused at the back door to allow his eyes to adjust to the bright afternoon light. The husky bartender was coming his way, up the path from the privy—even that was built out of adobe—that sat by the alley. "*Señor*, I have heard that you are looking for a cook."

"There are some men inside that are looking for some drinks." Fargo curbed his growing temper. "Shouldn't you tend to the job you've got now, instead of looking for a new one?"

"I am a great cook, *señor*. But alas, I have been reduced to—"

"Spare me the sad tale," Fargo grunted. "I'll come by here about an hour after sundown. You serve up your best dinner then, and if it tastes good to me, we'll talk about your future, understand?"

The bartender nodded, his face beaming as he went inside. Fargo took a few more steps. Before he could even think about climbing to the roof of the saloon, a gangly boy, running down the alley with a scrawny chicken tucked under one arm, hollered his way. "Hey, mister, you the one that's hiring for the government survey? I can do almost anything."

"Well, boy, it does look like you're good at foraging for food," Fargo conceded, annoyed by his sudden popularity in this town, where everybody seemed to be hungry and looking for a job.

The chicken pushed its head out and started squawking. The towheaded boy's eyes darted every which way as he tucked the fowl's head back into his armpit.

"You run along," Fargo advised, throwing the kid a quarter. "Go back the way you came. Use that money to square things with whoever owns the henhouse you just visited."

"What about . . ." the kid began to ask as he stared at his bare feet for a moment, then slowly turned to go back to what promised to be an embarrassing meeting.

"Find me tomorrow," Fargo ordered. He turned back to face the rear of the saloon. He decided he'd climb to its roof and creep forward to see what might be out in the street. It seemed sensible to be so cautious, because Doakes might be perched out there, waiting for him to emerge from the saloon's front door. Some folks were snoopy about the survey because they desperately wanted those dollar-a-day jobs.

But there were others who wanted to stop the survey. Why? Fargo couldn't come up with an answer there, although the how was becoming evident. Kill the guide, and the survey would be delayed until next summer, or maybe it would be canceled altogether. Zeb was dead, and now Fargo was the guide.

The adobe saloon building was only about ten feet high, but it was still difficult to get to the top. The cottonwood logs that held the roof in place stuck out in back, and by leaping, Fargo was able to grab one and pull himself up. A low barricade, about a foot high, stuck up in the front, and Fargo crawled behind it and got his pistol out before raising his head for a view.

Across the street sat a two-story frame hotel. He knew its layout fairly well, since that's where he had taken a room. In fact, he could look straight ahead and see right into his window.

More interesting, though, was the man sitting in the shade, on the full-length hotel porch. He looked a lot like Doakes, though he was older and his long beard was grizzled. At first, he seemed to be just another local idler who might soon be bothering Fargo for a job. The man appeared to be taking things easy in a rocking chair while he spit and whittled, sending streams of tobacco juice into the fresh pile of shavings he was creating.

Nothing else looked noteworthy, so Fargo studied the man on the porch. The more he saw, the less he liked. Most whittlers paid attention to their work, even if they were just whiling away an afternoon. But this man's eyes were on the saloon door. To make sure he didn't chop off any fingers on account of his inattention, he kept the blade at least six inches from where his left hand was holding the stick. The stick wasn't turning into anything. All that the man was making was shavings.

But if he was set up there to take a potshot at the Trailsman, where was his gun? Or would the man throw the knife he had at hand? But it was a considerable throw across the wide main street, and the knife had a thick, heavy haft. That made it ideal for whittling, but it was too unbalanced to throw well.

From below, Fargo heard the muffled sounds of an argument. It sounded as though the three drovers wanted to leave, and Captain Macomber was telling them to stay inside. The noises got louder, and something banged against the door.

The man across the street responded to the noise by rocking back, almost as far as the chair would go without tipping over, and loudly pounding the butt of the knife against the plank wall. The board must have been loose, because it sounded like a drum with a crisp rat-a-tat that carried easily to Fargo's ears.

Up in the Trailsman's room, a curtain fluttered. If it was a breeze, it was a peculiar breeze, because Fargo, only fifty feet away, hadn't felt any welcome puffs of air to carry off his sweat. He focused on the narrow, vertical window, which he had left open after checking in earlier today.

The gap between the two halves of the gray cotton curtain was only an inch or two wide, and the room was dark. Fargo stared intently, but he couldn't make out anything, not even the flowered design of the fly-specked wallpaper. But then he saw something moving slowly, about where a man's hands would be if he were standing next to the bed, where the Trailsman's gear was.

Some of this was starting to become clear. The man on the porch was a lookout. Whenever it seemed likely that someone might emerge from the saloon that Fargo had been sitting in, the whittler would pound on the wall. That would alert the prowler in the room. But what was the burglar looking for? Fargo carried his money with him, and most of his gear was stowed at the livery stable.

Getting some answers was going to be a major chore. Fargo could slide back, let himself down, get halfway across town so that he could cross the street without attracting notice, and then come up from the back way into the hotel. But in that fifteen or twenty minutes, the prowler and his lookout might vanish.

The Trailsman had already attracted some unwelcome attention from the local authorities, but still, a direct approach made sense. Best to double-check first, though. It was possible, although not likely, that the whittler was just that, and that the movement in his room was only the chambermaid.

Still lying prone, Fargo kicked at the roof. He heard some discussion downstairs, and the door below him began to open. The whittler rocked back and sent his staccato message. Over in his room, the curtains fluttered again.

Fargo had seen enough. He fired, sending a bullet into the hotel wall, just next to the window frame. He wanted to stir things up and see what happened.

His shot came as a total surprise to the whittler, who rocked back, thumped the wall, and then rolled down out of his chair so he could stay low if any more shots were fired. The thud of a saddlebag being dropped came from the Trailsman's room, followed by footsteps and a door being opened and closed.

Fargo watched the prone whittler as the slow steps came down the hotel's creaky stairs. The whittler obviously had planned on meeting his companion—Doakes the burglar—in back. But he didn't want to lift himself up and expose himself to another shot from somewhere across the street, either.

Now it was time to move. Fargo jumped off the roof, raising a cloud of dust as he landed on his feet. He had plunged only a dozen feet, but it was still far enough to make him wince and pause to catch his breath. "Stay put," he ordered the whittler.

The Trailsman then kicked back to force open the saloon door. "It's okay to come out now," he advised before sprinting across the street to the side of the hotel. Doakes would be coming out the back door any second now, and Fargo planned to meet him there with a Colt and some questions.

Revolver in hand, Fargo raced through the crowd that had gathered between the hotel and the adjacent millinery shop. When he reached the end of the hotel, he halted, then peered warily out into the alley. The most recent set of footprints went into the hotel's back door, so Doakes hadn't come out yet.

He heard some thumping from the front, maybe a signal from the lookout for Doakes to change directions. Fargo waited a moment, heard some footsteps inside head for the front, and went that way himself.

Just as he got to the front of the narrow passage he had just come down, the whittler arrived too, lunging at him with his knife.

Fargo dodged the blade, but that left him open for a savage uppercut that threatened to shake his teeth loose, if not shatter his jaw. It came close to knocking him out, and his opponent bulled on in, throwing Fargo's back to the ground while Doakes took off running.

Across the street, Macomber hollered at Doakes to halt. Since Doakes wasn't wearing a uniform, however, he didn't pay any attention to the captain's order. As Fargo tried to wrestle the knife away and bring his gun hand around to where it would do him some good, he caught a glimpse of the three drovers, all chasing after Doakes, with Macomber in the lead.

"I'm going to cut you up, you thieving bastard," the whittler grunted as he tried to bend his right arm toward the Trailsman. Fargo's clamp on the man's elbow kept the knife away, but not far enough away. Its tip was only inches from the Trailsman's chest. Fargo's other arm was stretched out on the street, held down by his opponent so that even though he could fire his pistol, he couldn't aim it to do any good.

"What'd I steal?" Fargo grunted. How could he get his gun around before his grip slackened on the arm and that wicked-looking knife sliced into his chest?

"Our map," his opponent answered. Then he sent a stream of tobacco juice onto the Trailsman's face.

Map? What map? Oh, shit, that piece of parchment that Zeb had passed along. It was sitting with his saddlebags over at the livery stable. Had anybody asked halfway politely for the supposed treasure map, Fargo probably would have given it away. But if somebody thought it was worth enough to be prowling and killing over, then maybe the map was worth looking at.

Enraged, Fargo shook the tobacco spittle from his face and put every ounce of muscle into shoving that knife back. The man's strong arm yielded a few inches, giving the Trailsman some room to buck upward. That rattled the whittler, who had to shift. The pressure momentarily eased on Fargo's gun arm.

Fargo used that moment to snap his Colt to his side and jam the muzzle against the man's hip. "Feel this?" Fargo muttered. "Now back off."

"Hell, no," came the answer, along with a powerful effort to send the knife toward Fargo's heaving chest. When the man started to spit again, Fargo sent a bullet into the man's ass. He pitched forward in shock. Fargo's grip on the knife arm was strong enough to roll the bleeding, thrashing man off him.

The man was alive enough to lunge for Fargo as the Trailsman got to his feet, but a boot in the ribs settled him down some.

"Tell me about the map you say I stole." Fargo stood two paces back as he covered the writhing man with his pistol.

"Doakes told me it was his, that he came by it honestly. He said that Zeb Reynolds stole it from him, and you killed Zeb for it. He wanted me to help him get it back."

"You know Doakes?"

"Used to ride with him. Hadn't seen him for a while until he showed up here a couple days ago." He collected his breath. "Sorry I spit at you."

Fargo reined in his anger. Considering what this man had been told, he probably felt justified in showing such contempt for the Trailsman. "Okay, you're sorry." Fargo turned on his heel.

"Wait, mister."

"Why?"

"It was just a flesh wound you gave me. I'll be up and going in no time at all."

"So?"

"So, do you think you'll need to hire a striker? I can do almost any odd job that needs to be done."

Fargo shrugged and walked down the street to the barbershop, where a hot bath cost a whole dime but was worth it.

4

For the past two weeks, there hadn't been enough surveying done to make a difference. Granted, at every campsite the surveyors had set up their equipment, but they just took a few readings and made some notes, and that was it.

Occupied with the demands of getting a bunch of strangers—both people and livestock—to travel together efficiently and harmoniously, the Trailsman hadn't yet found time to satisfy his curiosity about the surveyors' work. Picking up a crew in the Pueblo had been easy enough, although Fargo felt badly about not being able to hire everyone who wanted a job. A lot of them needed the work, if there was any truth in all those stories about widowed mothers with big families to feed, farms eaten out by grasshoppers, and cattle operations that didn't need stock tenders anymore because raiding Utes had stolen their herds.

But Fargo felt satisfied with his crew. Lank Hobbs was as good as wranglers came, and he and his two friends got along with the other three Fargo had hired. Pedro Romero's cooking was a bit on the spicy side, perhaps, but sooner or later those complaining New Englanders would realize that they were in the West, where nobody else could tolerate the insipid taste of the boiled beef they liked so much.

Out of habit, Fargo scanned the countryside. They had proceeded west, up the Arkansas until they struck

Hardscrabble Creek, and veered south. As Fargo recalled, the narrow valley had held a few farms, but those had been abandoned after numerous Ute raids. At the head of Hardscrabble Creek, they dropped into a wide, mountain-rimmed valley, so high and cool that the grass remained green and lush, even this late in the summer. The jagged north end of the Sangre de Cristo range rose to his right. Over to the left, the smaller and rounder Wet Mountains separated them from the Great Plains.

Their immediate destination was Fort Garland, on the other side of the Sangres, and Fargo knew he would soon have to decide which trail to take. He had hoped the trail would help him make that decision—if there was Indian sign on a given route, that was ample reason to take another—but it appeared that his party was the first to come through since the last good rain, several days ago.

From his usual place at the vanguard, a quarter-mile ahead of the wending pack train, Fargo reined up and looked back. He'd only have to wait a few minutes for Captain Macomber to catch up.

The captain often rode with Sergeant O'Reilly, the quartermaster, but today O'Reilly was back with the wranglers, who handled the pack train and the loose stock at the rear. In between were the surveyors and their helpers, a bunch of tight-mouthed, snooty complainers whom Fargo would never please, unless he found some way to pack featherbeds and entire libraries atop the narrow backs of the mules, which were, in comparison to the surveyors at least, downright cooperative and friendly.

"Today's the day we've got to decide which route to take to Garland," Fargo told Macomber as the officer arrived.

"As long as we get there, I suppose it's up to you to decide how," the captain replied, pausing to rub the stubble on his face. Just yesterday, he had decided that the customary morning shave was too much trouble, especially when mirrors were so scarce that everybody had to share one.

"I thought so." Fargo stretched, then pointed to several low spots in the towering wall of gray mountains that loomed to the west. "There are four passes, more or less. Due west is Music Pass, with Medano a bit south."

Macomber squinted into the sun and nodded before the Trailsman continued.

"The next gap is Mosca Pass. The big hump is Blanca Peak, which keeps you from seeing Sangre de Cristo Pass. Any of them will get us to Garland well enough. Just wanted to know if you had a preference, that's all."

The captain thought it over for a bit. "Seems to me that I read in Zebulon Pike's journal that there are some big sand dunes that run for miles over on the other side of Medano Pass. Traipsing through sand is hard on mules, with their narrow hooves, so if I had a preference, it would be for one of the others."

Macomber's direct knowledge of the country he surveyed was scanty, almost nonexistent. But the captain had done his best to prepare by reading every journal he could find. Fargo didn't like reading about the territory, especially when the accounts were so fanciful, with more bragging and bullshit than what you heard around campfires when a jug was going around, but he found himself respecting Macomber for his efforts.

"Music and Mosca also run into those dunes," Fargo explained, "so Sangre de Cristo Pass makes sense to me, too. It drops over to the south of the sand piles. The trail damn near runs into Fort Garland's parade ground." Fargo stood in his stirrups and twisted back; the train had almost caught up to them.

"Sangre it is," Macomber decided.

Fargo kneed the Ovaro forward, and Macomber rode abreast, instead of staying back with the train.

"Why's it so important to get to Garland? We're in good shape on supplies," Fargo inquired.

"When the army closed Fort Massachusetts in '58 and moved a few miles south to set up at Garland," Macomber explained, "they did a very precise survey, running chains and lines all the way north from Santa Fe. They tied a monument at Garland to the New Mexico Principal Meridian. That's a known spot that ties to all our maps, so that's where we start looking like surveyors."

"I wondered why nobody had been running lines or anything like that. They just check the odometer and take sightings when we set up camp. I'd have asked one of them, but they all think they're too good to talk to some rough-edged frontiersman that didn't go to college."

"Well, all they're doing now is mapping this road, where it fords creeks and so forth. Between their star sightings at night, and the odometer and compass readings during the day, they can figure out enough to put this road onto the official maps."

Fargo shrugged. This trail had been around for as long as white men had been visiting the territory, connecting the traders' settlement known as the Pueblo to the real pueblos down by Taos. Back in 1779, Juan Batista de Anza, the Spanish governor of what was now New Mexico, had used this route to return home after riding north with his own soldiers and some Ute allies to punish Comanche raiders. It was known to other Indians—the Navaho and the Jicarilla Apaches—and before them, to the wandering buffalo. None of them needed the assurance or guidance of an official map to get from one place to another. But none of them had gone to college, either.

Fargo had been warned about that before hiring on as the guide, so he didn't have any real cause to complain. It wouldn't have done any good anyway. Better to think about his end of things, which was to continue south until he spotted a good campsite, close by the eastern foot of Sangre de Cristo Pass.

There wasn't anything wrong with the place he found.

It had water, wood, and ample forage. There wasn't any Indian sign, although that didn't mean much. They were in Jicarilla Apache country now.

All other known bands of Apache frequented the deserts to the southwest. The Jicarilla—the name meant "basket-makers"—lived up here, where forested mountains met emerald valleys, and they lived like the Plains tribes, with tepees instead of hogans. But the Jicarilla were still Apache, which meant they were sneaky, so good at hiding themselves that a man could never be sure that they weren't around, ready to slink in and ride off with goods or livestock.

Once camp was set up, Fargo found Lank Hobbs, who spoke little but was still better company than anybody else around. "You ever trail through here before?"

Hobbs nodded. "Cattle a time or two." He returned his attention to his tin cup of strong black coffee.

"Ever get raided?" Sometimes it was exasperating to talk to Hobbs. The taciturn drover would answer your questions straight enough, but he never volunteered a syllable more than a precise answer.

The lean cowboy shook his head. "Nope."

Fargo wanted to grab the man and shake some information out of him, but knew it wouldn't do any good. Best to be patient. He could read concern in Hobbs' gray eyes, and he wanted to know if those concerns were the same as his.

"Lank, you think there's a chance we might get hit here? We're in Jicarilla country, and the only bigger thieves are the Utes and the Comanches, who also wander around here from time to time."

Maybe the Trailsman's intense look was having an effect on the cowboy's laconic nature, for his reply seemed almost wordy. "Not to mention assorted outlaw bands from New Mexico, which aren't all that far south." Hobbs grinned and brought Fargo a cup of coffee.

"Then we'd better set up some guards tonight. Who's turn is it to nighthawk?"

Lank pointed to a towheaded kid whose hair showed copper red, even through the dust. He was sitting by the fire, gulping coffee and still trying to wake up, even though he had just done some hard and fast riding. The nighthawk bedded down in the morning, and he always had a good horse, so that early in the afternoon, he could wake and then catch up to the others. Since nobody much cared for the job, it was usually rotated among the group.

"Little Red there," Lank drawled. "Always his turn. He up and volunteered for it first night and said he'd be proud to do it every night from then on." Lank paused and took a sip of coffee before proceeding. "Nobody seemed all that eager to fight him for that chore, so the rest of us get to sleep regular hours."

Fargo stepped over to the campfire. The drovers grudgingly agreed that, now that they were in Indian country, a night guard made sense. Before they could draw straws to see who'd stand guard, though, Little Red protested.

"We haven't had a bit of trouble so far, and you yourself said you didn't see any Indian sign, Mr. Fargo. From what I've heard, if there was any to be seen, you'd be the one to see it. You think I can't do the job?"

"Didn't say that," Fargo intoned.

"Well, that's what I'm hearing," Red piped. He couldn't be much more than sixteen or seventeen, though he was talking bigger. "If trouble comes during the night, I'll sure as hell rouse this camp. But if it doesn't, which is the likely case, why for should all the other hands get their sleep messed up?" He sounded pretty vehement and the others looked hopeful of getting to sleep through the night.

Fargo shrugged. "Okay, Red. You do it the usual way. But if anything's missing, come morning, it'll come out of your hide, hear?"

Red nodded an assurance that all would be in order, and the others looked glad enough not to have to stand night guard in shifts.

Fargo didn't stay in his bedroll, though. As usual, he set up about a hundred yards from the main camp. That way, if strangers should sneak up, there was a chance of catching them in a cross fire. It sometimes made for lonely trips, but it went with the job.

He was surprised by how much activity there was around camp when he slithered out of his bedroll, sometime around midnight. Most people were bedded down and snoring away, but Red was off with the mules, far downstream. Fargo could hear him making horseback rounds and sometimes singing to himself. On a rise close to camp, the eminent astronomer and surgeon, Kaspar Krantz, had set up some of his equipment beneath a black sky full of twinkling stars. Right next to him, one of the chainmen held a notebook, along with a tin-and-glass lantern that had a smoking tallow candle inside.

"Ah, our esteemed guide." Krantz didn't sound condescending or sarcastic, so Fargo asked him what they were up to.

"We are shooting the north star tonight, as we must do several times during every night." He paused, looked into the eyepiece, and made some adjustments.

"I can see shooting it once," Fargo said after the scientist straightened. "That'd give you your direction, and you'd get our latitude from the polestar's elevation, right?"

Krantz nodded. "For general work, that would be sufficient. But we need to be more precise, and that requires many sightings, for the polestar is not exactly where it should be."

"It's above the north pole, isn't it?"

"Close, but not quite." Krantz seemed to welcome this opportunity to explain his work to someone who found it new and interesting, instead of boring and routine. "The earth spins, as you know, and it wobbles just a bit."

"Like a spinning top?"

"Precisely. It is the same force that accounts for

both. But at any rate, Polaris is at due north only twice a day. As we see it, it swings east and west. It doesn't move much, less than the eye can detect, which is why we need these instruments. But we must take several readings, spaced hours apart, and average those to establish the true north and the true latitude. One reading is more than enough to point a man in the right direction, but on these land maps, we could be off by a mile or more if we did not take these measurements."

"Does sound like a lot of trouble for you, Doctor Krantz." Fargo gained respect for the man who had always seemed so tired and lethargic during the day. It was no wonder, if he'd been getting up every couple hours each night to look at the stars.

"It is indeed," Krantz agreed. "But I am teaching Mr. Robards here how this is done, so that I can enjoy a decent night's sleep from time to time."

The thin-faced chainman stifled a shiver—these mountains were cold at night, even in the summer—and shuffled things around enough so that he could shake Fargo's hand. "Virgil Robards, sir," he offered.

Fargo returned the handshake. It was strange, finally managing to be introduced, after they'd been traveling together for two weeks. But the surveyors kept to themselves, and hell, it was their party. Fargo was just a hired man.

"I suppose you guys will want to catch a nap now." Fargo began to step back.

"Don't you want to know what we do with the north once we have it?"

"Sure," Fargo granted. "Most mornings, I've seen stakes in the ground that run north and south."

"We set those at night," Robards explained. "Then we use that line to find out the correction for our compasses, since magnetic north is not the same as due north, except in a few places. If we stay in one place for a day, we can determine true solar noon, when the shadow falls into line, and that way we can set our watches accurately. If only there was a way to make our barometers—"

He quieted at Fargo's hush. Something was moving near camp. It was downstream, near the mules.

"I'm obliged for the science lesson," Fargo whispered. "You men have any weapons?"

Robards produced a derringer. It could shoot accurately for at least a yard, but it would make enough noise to rouse the camp.

"Keep it handy. I think we have some company tonight."

It was more the prickly feeling on the back of his neck than the sound of movement that bothered Fargo as he padded, deliberately and noiselessly, toward the mules. They were pastured along the creek, and the sounds were from above. Just what was he hearing?

Nothing serious. Just some footsteps and some grass tearing, the way calves sounded when they were eating at night. Then it struck him that they didn't have any cattle. That was an old Apache trick, pulling up clumps of grass so that the sound would cover up any untoward noises.

Fargo moved closer, rounding the bend. Beneath the starlight, the mules and the few riding horses milled nervously, long slender mule ears poking into the night. Where was Red, the nighthawk?

Nowhere to be seen, but that wasn't saying much, because there wasn't much Fargo could see. But he was damn sure that raiders were creeping up on the herd.

A man on foot could get trampled if these animals stampeded, which might happen any second, but there wasn't time to saddle the Ovaro. Fargo cursed, then knelt, to keep himself low, and whistled for the Ovaro.

The big pinto seemed a bit agitated as Fargo rolled aboard, bareback. He lay flat, his head pressed against the horse's neck, as he sorted out sounds, straining to hear over the horse's heartbeat and his own pounding pulse.

Four of them, Fargo decided, two on each side of the herd. Two were on the hillside, and the other two were back, toward the creek. They were moving with due stealth, but Fargo pinpointed them, once he knew what to listen for. They would creep ever closer to the herd, then vault aboard the nearest animals bareback. With some whoops and shouts, they would cause a stampede, leaving the survey party stranded.

The sounds came closer and then some owls started hooting back and forth at one another. Since there weren't any trees close by, the hoots had to be signals that the Jicarilla were passing back and forth. Fargo didn't know the code, so he couldn't tell which one would be the signal to begin. All he could do was guess by the distance of the hoots. He wanted the Indians to be almost in the herd when he made his move.

Out of the darkness came two long hoots, followed by a short answer, but Fargo had heard that signal before. The signal to begin would be something new, he felt certain. Three longs sounded, and he straightened and waved his hat with several shouts, as shrill as he could make his deep voice go. The already-nervous herd began to step downhill, toward the tree-lined creek. Fargo let loose with a precious round from his Colt, not caring whether the star he pointed at was due north or not.

That was enough to inspire the mules and horses. They lifted their tails and began to run. Even the Ovaro wanted to join the bustling crowd, and without a bridle or saddle, Fargo didn't have much choice but to go along for the ride.

He heard one unseen man's moan as he tried to grab a fleeing mule and got nothing but a handful of mane. Another emitted an anguished wail when hurried hooves bowled him over and pounded him into the grass. In the middle of the herd, he urged the Ovaro forward. Fargo pushed for the front, where he could turn the leaders so that the mules would begin to circle.

So intent was he on turning the mules that he didn't notice, not soon enough anyway, that one of the mules had a rider. Under the stars, all he saw was the motion when the man straightened. Since there wasn't any saddle on that mule, Fargo knew the rider couldn't be Red.

Fargo started to bring up his pistol when the Ovaro pitched after almost losing a hoof down a marmot hole. The other man, about ten yards away and clutching a mule's mane with his left hand, took the first shot.

Even though the man was shooting in almost total darkness while atop a frightened mule, the shot passed close enough for the bullet's hot breath to wash against Fargo's ear. Fargo stayed low until he was certain of his shot. His bullet slammed into the rider's neck, pitching the man sideways as he struggled to stay aboard, above those thrashing hooves below. The round must have smashed an artery, because blood, just a black outline against the low stars to the south, sprayed out in all directions, as if something had exploded.

Horseflesh hated the scent of fresh blood, though, so there wasn't much hope of turning this herd now. Fargo bent low and held on, trying to gather his wits.

There had been four men sneaking up on the herd, and he knew what had happened to three of them. Fargo lifted his head to see where the herd was going. The noise told him that they were almost at the rocky creek. The herd would turn there, and Fargo would try to make the animals veer toward camp. Sending animals uphill is one way to make them lose enthusiasm, and besides, the mules wouldn't want to run straight into camp. That might be enough to make them slow down.

But the mules and horses pounded around the bend, and Fargo realized that if they didn't slow down shortly, the whole sleeping survey party would get trampled.

Up on the hillside above camp, Fargo saw the tiny candle lantern. He hollered, hoping his voice would carry above the hooves.

A shot from the derringer responded. For a moment, the herd didn't know which way to go as the leaders shied and lost interest in galloping any farther. Still, they were close, and the animals in the back reared, bit, and thrashed, shoving the herd forward.

Fargo looked back as the last few animals rounded the bend. There was a waving hat atop a horse, and Red's tinny voice was shouting, urging the animals on. Next to him was another set of waving hands and an agitated voice.

What was Red doing back there, stampeding the herd? Fargo didn't know and didn't want to wait for an answer. The survey party was starting to come to life, as the furious thrashing hooves came within a hundred yards of camp. The derringer on the hillside went off again, providing some help as the noise frightened the leaders into shying back.

From amid those leaders, Fargo added his own shot, toward the only stampeder he could see. He hoped it was that turncoat bastard Red, but he didn't really care which man it was that fell to the ground, a gaping hole in his chest.

5

"You can put that thing back in your holster, Fargo. It makes me edgy as hell." Lank's agitated features showed that he was telling the truth about his taut nerves as the head wrangler and his companions stood on one side of the rekindled campfire, facing Fargo.

Once awakened by the tumult of hooves pounding toward them, the stock tenders had roused instantly to help get the mule herd settled down. Fargo wanted some answers, though, and it was too dark to go looking, so he started asking questions.

"I don't know who's trustworthy here and who isn't. Tell me about Little Red."

Lank gulped some cold night air. "Not a lot to tell. He showed up back at the Pueblo, after you hired me as the wrangler, and I was puttin' together a crew. It was obvious that he knew how to handle the herd so I asked you to hire him."

"Had you ever seen him before?"

Lank thought. Behind him, there was quite a bit of noise as the surveyors and helpers, still bedded down, complained about getting their sleep interrupted.

"That I had, now and again. He rode for an outfit over in the San Luis Valley, and sometimes he was with 'em when they'd trail some of their cattle to the Pueblo. He wasn't a total stranger, but I can't say we were good buddies, either. He seemed to know his work well enough."

Fargo relaxed and eased the Colt back into its holster, although he still kept his right hand on its butt. "So it came as a surprise to you, too, when Red turned out to be working against us, not for us."

"Wasn't my idea to steal our mules," Lank agreed. "Especially not by working with redskins."

From up on the hillside, someone approached the fire, moving lightly like a person accustomed to walking around in the dark. Fargo recognized the voice—it belonged to Virgil Robards, the chainman who had been helping the astronomer.

Still watching Lank and the other wranglers from the corner of his eye, Fargo turned to face Robards. "That was you firing that derringer up there?"

The lean-faced youth nodded. "I was aiming at the stars. I hoped that the flash or the noise might frighten those mules and discourage them from trampling our camp. Wasn't that the right thing to do?"

"Might have been what made the difference," Fargo complimented. "Have you been looking at the sky every night?"

Robards nodded and looked around the fire, obviously hoping that somebody had put on some coffee, but there wasn't any.

"Did you ever see Red doing anything unusual at night?" Fargo asked.

The chainman fiddled with the buttons on his jacket for a tense minute or so. "Usually the herd was kept some distance from camp, Mr. Fargo, and my mind was on the heavens, not the earth. But, yes, there was a peculiar event two nights ago. I got the impression that four or five horsemen were coming to our camp to meet with Red at night."

"Impression?"

"Muffled sounds, and I could discern their shapes from time to time."

"You didn't tell me about this?"

"I didn't know you well enough to feel comfortable talking to you at all, Mr. Fargo. You're not an easy man to approach."

Fargo felt exactly the same way about the surveyors, who always talked among themselves, and if they had anything to say to him, it was relayed through Captain Macomber. When people traveled together, though, that sort of formalized communication could lead to problems; it already had.

"The way I read things," Fargo explained, "somebody is hell-bent on stopping this survey, though I don't have the vaguest idea as to why. But they planted Red among our crew."

"You sure Red was part of it?" Lank protested. He'd been the one who wanted Red, so it was understandable that he was pushing this way.

"Damn sure," Fargo grunted. "Didn't he get upset last night when we offered him help with the nighthawk job? Didn't he say he'd rather be out there by himself?"

"You mean . . ." Lank stopped, not liking what he was thinking. "You mean that Red didn't want any help from us because he had some help comin' from outside, tryin' to swipe our herd?"

"Looks that way."

"That son of a bitch. Where is he? I'll take a horsewhip to him, and then we can string him up properly, as soon as we find a decent tree." Lank turned and spit.

"I don't know just where he was when the dust settled. There were at least four others, likely Utes, since Jicarilla aren't quite so cooperative," Fargo explained. "Once we get some sunlight, it'll be easier to sort things out. But till then, we're just going to have to watch and wait."

At Lank's order, the drovers began to saddle up, over by the fire, where there was some hope of seeing what they were doing. By then, Pedro had risen, and the good-natured cook tended to his first chore: getting the men filled up with strong black coffee.

Fargo decided to walk up to the astronomer's outdoor observatory, figuring he could see stars from just about anywhere, but the hillside perch would let him know if anything developed down below. Steaming cup of coffee in hand, he was halfway up the rock-strewn hillock when he heard the Ovaro's nicker among the wranglers' muttered curses about Red's perfidy.

He turned and stared back toward camp. Looking like phantoms in the starlight, the shadowy wranglers were pushing the horseflesh back where it belonged, about a mile downstream, around a bend. The Ovaro would be in that herd, and Fargo finally made out his familiar form, toward the back, and still nickering from time to time.

In camp, Pedro had the fire built up. The cook sat close by, mixing flour, water, salt, and bacon grease. Once the dough was ready, he'd set a piece of sheet iron over the fire to cook the breakfast tortillas. Tortillas were a lot like regular griddle cakes, except they were flatter and crisper. Fargo didn't see much reason to pick one over the other, but you'd have thought Pedro was trying to poison them, the way some of the surveyors complained about the unfamiliar meals.

Pedro's victims slumbered to the Trailsman's right, some in conical canvas tents, and a few daring to sleep under the stars. Directly past Pedro, toward the willow-lined creek, most of the gear sat in neat piles, behind a row of packsaddles.

Pedro rose, apparently to get something. He stepped out of the ring of light, and Fargo's eyes took several moments to adjust.

Something was moving by the gear. It could have been just a pack rat, flitting from morsel to morsel. Maybe it was a porcupine, looking for a sweat-soaked tail strap to gnaw on. Or it could be a man. Fargo couldn't be sure. All he saw was motion.

The kneeling Trailsman rose and drained his coffee with one swig. He wanted to race down the hillside, but that was pure foolishness in the dark.

Fargo covered as much ground as he felt he safely could. The cook was almost to the gear, close to where that motion had been.

"Pedro, wait up a minute," Fargo boomed.

The stocky cook's shuffle slowed but did not halt. "What is it that you need, Señor Fargo? Isn't your coffee strong enough?"

"Just stand still," Fargo commanded, gaining speed as he reached the flat.

His order came too late. Pedro had reached the canvas panniers that held his cooking gear. He tugged at a cover strap, anxious to get it open so he could grab whatever he had come for and go back to work.

While Pedro bent over and the Trailsman ran toward him, the shape on the far side of the saddles began to slither downstream. When the cook swung the pannier back, he froze. He saw that the shape was a human form, and moments later, it began to rise.

Fargo didn't see the knife in the man's hand, but he figured that anybody skulking around like that, especially on a night like this, couldn't be up to any good. On the run, he drew his Colt and fired.

His hurried shot missed, the bullet flying harmlessly into the willows, but it sent the shadow back down. Pedro, too, went down in a face-first sprawl. Fargo couldn't tell whether the unarmed cook was just being sensible or whether he had been wounded by a knife thrown by that sneaking phantom.

Only yards away, he halted and looked hard, trying to discern his quarry amid the gear. Pedro got up on all fours and lunged toward a gap between saddles. From the darkness, Fargo caught the glint of firelight on cold steel.

The Trailsman instantly moved sideways, cursing himself as the fire's orange glow fell upon him. He knew better than to stand near the fire, where his looming silhouette presented a considerable temptation. Luckily, the razor-tipped knife merely sliced through the flying tail of his jacket.

The shadow popped up again. Before Fargo could fire, Pedro launched a flying tackle that sent both tumbling into the gear, with the clatter of tools banging one another and the tinkle of fragile instruments getting knocked around. The instruments were vital, but they could be repaired and adjusted, even replaced if they were damaged beyond repair. The cook probably felt differently about whether he could be replaced if he got damaged that much.

Unable to see what he was doing, Fargo pawed at the thrashing legs and grabbed a moccasined foot. One of Pedro's heaving boots caught him in the jaw, but Fargo didn't think the cook meant anything personal by that. The Trailsman got both hands on the moccasin-clad foot and began to twist with such force that either the shadowy intruder would roll off Pedro, or his ankle would snap.

Both men grunted and panted in short, labored breaths. From out of nowhere, the Indian's foot slammed into Fargo's groin. Doubled over and fighting his pain and anger, Fargo increased the twist on the foot he held. He heard a fist slam against a jaw, and from the moan, he knew that Pedro had been on the receiving end.

Fargo hooked his heels into the ground for some support and jerked hard at the foot he had, hoping to pull the invader out away from Pedro. But the muscled attacker had other ideas and clung to Pedro. Then the man gasped. Moments later, his muscles relaxed, and Pedro began to stand. Fargo tugged and was rewarded by a sickening charnel cascade of slimy and still-throbbing intestines.

Just a moment earlier, Pedro had managed to plant a foot-long butcher knife somewhere near the Indian's navel. He had worked the knife up, clear to the brisket, before the Ute marauder had given up. At least he looked Ute, once they brought over a firebrand, although there was so much blood and spilled guts that it was hard to tell.

"So that is why you wanted me to halt before I reached the pannier," Pedro muttered, wiping his hands on his spattered canvas apron.

"Saw something moving down there, but I wasn't sure what it was," Fargo explained.

"It's a good thing I was going over to get a knife, not a bowl." Pedro chuckled. "Was he part of the other raid?"

Fargo shrugged. "Don't know. Stands to reason that the rustlers working with Red were Utes, but until there's some more light so we can find the bodies and take a look at them, your guess is as good as mine."

A guttural shout from Doctor Krantz, a quarter-mile away, caught Fargo's attention, but he didn't know what the astronomer was saying. Fargo spun around, saw the warning flash from the derringer up there, and hit the ground, moments before Pedro landed next to him, amid the Ute's still-warm entrails. A bullet whistled overhead, but it came from downstream, not from that little derringer way up there.

Now a gray hint of light made a halo around Greenhorn Peak to the east. Fargo wiped the splashed blood out of his eyes, shook some more off his head, and squinted toward the source of the gunshot. Damn. It had come from the far side of the camp. Tents obscured what little view he had, and people were starting to stir. If any of the awakening survey party sat up, they'd be easy targets, and Fargo had the idea that whoever was shooting didn't care whom he hit, just as long as the shot discouraged the surveyors.

As if to confirm the Trailsman's surmise, the next bullet plowed into a bedroll, sending up a cloud of lint, followed by an anguished howl of pain that rose at the same time as blood gushed up from a smashed artery. Fargo sent a shot back that way, hoping to buy himself the time he'd need.

"Get your pistol, Pedro." Fargo flitted his eyes that way and saw that the cook was already crawling toward the fire, where the butt of a long-barreled dragoon pistol stuck out of a washpan. "Give me some cover."

"Sí," Pedro shouted, hoping to draw the shooter's attention so that the man wouldn't be murdering people in their sleep.

As soon as Pedro got within reach of the pistol, Fargo stood up and took off running, zigzagging along the line of packsaddles. Whoever had been wounded in camp was trying to stay quiet about it, although there were still the anguished sounds that an injured man made when he tried to breathe through clenched teeth.

With every step, Fargo got closer. In the hushed gray of dawn, he could already discern the darker haze of powder smoke, just on the other side of a tent. And, dammit, somebody in the canvas structure stood up, bumping against its sloping roof, which inspired a shot into the wall from the unseen intruder.

Fargo could hardly fire back through the tent. "Get your asses down," he shouted, "and keep them there."

The next bullet came within inches of an axman's head, then hit a rock and ricocheted. The howling lead disk barely cleared Fargo's leg, but he felt better when he heard Pedro's big pistol roar once and roar again.

Trying not to step on people, but not caring much whether he did, Fargo raced to the tent and around it, Colt before him.

There was Red, perched on one knee, both hands on his revolver as he set up for a forty-yard shot at Pedro. That would have been a tough shot for any man with a pistol, even the Trailsman, but Fargo decided not to give Red a chance. Fargo's slug caught Red at the base of his skull.

The turncoat nighthawk pitched forward a bit. His head snapped up and then his face exploded. Between his shattered skull and the eviscerated Ute, this was starting to look more like a shambles than a survey camp.

Now that there was decent light, though, there shouldn't be any new bloodshed. Nighttime raiders, if there were any left, tended to disappear when the darkness did.

"It's okay to start getting up," Fargo announced to the sprawling group as he stepped over to the wounded man, grabbing a canteen on the way.

He grasped the slim hand and helped the man—he wasn't really much more than a boy—to sit up, still in the bloodstained bedroll. "Where'd you get hit?"

"My right limb" was the breathy reply.

"High or low?"

"Pardon?"

"Above the knee or below? Did it break anything, or was it just a flesh wound?" Fargo brought the canteen up to the pale lips while the injured lad glared at him.

"My tibia has been punctured, I believe."

For all that Fargo could tell, the kid's brains must have been damaged. Maybe there were times to be prim and proper, but this sure wasn't one of them. It didn't look like the wound was still bleeding, although everything was still tucked inside the bedroll, so Fargo stood up and spotted Krantz, who was supposed to be a surgeon as well as an astronomer.

Krantz understood that the tibia was what anybody sensible would call a shinbone, and he went over to the gear to fetch his black bag. He paused to give the gutted Indian a cursory look-over.

Fargo's stomach-turning examination took a bit longer. It wasn't too hard to tell Utes from Jicarilla Apache, although they dressed alike. Apache never braided their blue-black hair. But the Horse Utes and the Comanche, although usually at war with one another, were kin. Their languages were similar and the men of both tribes tended to be barrel-shaped and bowlegged.

The blood-spattered beadwork on the dead warrior's vest made a stylized picture of several tepees and horses, along with pine trees and a mountain or two. Since the colors were mostly turquoise and crimson, the vest had started as the handiwork of a Hunkpapa Sioux woman. The pattern on the elkhide moccasins was just that, a pattern that didn't resemble anything in nature, and the background beadwork was tan, not white, so the footwear was Cheyenne, not

Arapaho. The breeching was just trade cloth from Santa Fe, and it looked Navaho. Comanche were too close-minded to be wearing such a variety of stolen or traded clothing, so this dead warrior must have been Ute.

The other two dusky corpses looked much the same. One of last night's raiders had been wounded, but managed to crawl off. Fargo decided he'd better follow that up before the fleeing man alerted the rest of his band, but that could wait until he'd had a chance to examine what was left of Red.

Macomber had beat him to it. As Fargo stepped up, the captain was adding the contents of Red's butternut shirt pocket to the little pile of stuff he'd found in Red's pants. Fargo knelt and sorted through it. The only item of any value was a cheap brass pocket watch, which still ticked. There were a few lucifers in a waterproof case, a penknife, and a tin that held a few percussion caps. But the tin looked familiar—just like one of the Trailsman's, though such containers were hardly rarities. Had Red been rifling through Fargo's gear during some night while he snored?

That question was answered when Macomber stripped the shirt off the corpse. Tucked beneath it was a folded chunk of cream-colored parchment, about a foot square when Macomber opened it.

"That's mine," Fargo interjected.

"You shot him. To the victor goes the spoils." Macomber smiled. "Looks like some kind of map," he added as he passed the chart to Fargo's waiting fingers.

"I suppose that's what it is." The writing was some sort of convoluted script, so he couldn't be sure which way was up as he examined the thing for the first time. "You folks are the experts on maps, so maybe you can make heads or tails of it. I can't even read the words."

Macomber sidled next to Fargo and squinted. "Rotate it," he urged. Fargo complied. "The writing's in Latin cursive. I'd guess it was a priest's and that it was written about a century ago. But that's just guessing. You have any idea where it came from?"

Fargo remained silent for a minute, amid the general noise of a day getting under way. He decided to tell Macomber as much as he knew about the map, which wasn't much: just what Zeb had said, and how a lot of folks seemed to want the map enough to take up killing.

While Macomber thought that over and deciphered a few words that indicated mountains and creeks, Fargo looked hard at the fading brown ink. A sawtooth line seemed to indicate a ridge. Near the center of the ridge was a Maltese cross, a plus sign with flared ends. An inch or so closer were some lines that might mean a cliff, and below the cliff was a creek that meandered above and below, but ran straight when it passed through a gorge. By the cross, there were arrows and numbers, along with several words, which might be distances and directions to certain landmarks.

But that was just conjecture, and even if he had been absolutely certain as to what those symbols represented, all Fargo knew was that the map represented someplace in the mountains. Since there were chains and ranges of mountains just about anywhere one cared to look, that wasn't a lot of help.

"Think it's a treasure map?" Macomber wondered.

"So the tale goes."

"I've heard my share and more of stories about conquistadors who found gold and were attacked and had to cache it before they could get back to the settled parts of Mexico," the captain agreed. "But this map may have some truth behind it."

"Why's that?"

"Well, in my line of work, dealing with these land grants, I get to see a lot of old Mexican maps, because we have to work from them sometimes. And this one looks authentic."

"You mean people forge them?"

Macomber laughed. "Hell, yes. And then they come up with some crazy story about how the map they just drew points straight to Montezuma's lost treasures. Of course, the man with the map always has some problem that keeps him from going out to claim the treasure himself. But he'll be glad to sell that precious map to you."

Now that Fargo thought about it, he remembered a few saloon offers of such maps. Being a man who didn't have much use for maps of any sort, Fargo had just passed them over. "But you don't think this is one of those fake maps?"

Macomber shook his head. "I can't say it's genuine. But it looks right. And whoever drew it knew enough to write 'aurum' instead of 'gold' or 'oro' on a map that's supposed to be in Latin."

Fargo chuckled. "Guess that would be a dead giveaway." His sober tone returned. "Wish I knew what to do with it."

"Aren't you going to keep it?"

"Guess so." Fargo rose and wished he had some coffee. He started toward the fire, and Macomber joined his steps. "Trouble is, this map doesn't do me a bit of good, since I've got no idea how that area fits into the big scheme of things. Even worse, there are folks trying to get it from me—any way they can. Somebody put Red up to swiping it, probably the same people that arranged for this Indian raid, with him helping on the inside. So as long as I've got that map, I'm a target. If I just threw it in the fire now, I'd still be a target. Old Zeb sure didn't do me any favors when he passed on that map."

Macomber surveyed the camp. Everybody was up and dressed, most had eaten, and the wranglers were bringing up the mules for the start of today's packing.

Fargo turned to the captain. "Think you can handle the guiding today?"

"Certainly, Mr. Fargo. But why?"

"The only answers I'm going to get will come from the closest band of Utes. So if you can get your party started up the pass—there's a camping spot on your left, about fifteen miles up, just below timberline—then I'm going to go see some Utes today."

Macomber grimaced. "Wouldn't it be safer to send a courier over to Garland and come back with a cavalry escort?"

"I just want a friendly conversation," Fargo explained, "and when you ride in with the Blue Sleeves, redskins are seldom friendly."

Macomber nodded, then grimaced even worse when Fargo stepped over to the gutted Indian, pulled out his belt knife, then knelt and started peeling off the scalp. The surveyors looked disgusted, too.

But Lank Hobbs understood and appeared with a bloody ring of braided black hair from downstream, where he'd been pushing the mules forward. If you wanted to talk seriously with Indians, they had to respect you. The dusky Horse Utes were warriors, and the more fresh scalps you toted, the more respect you got. Since nobody objected, Fargo even added Red's shoulder-length locks, which were the color of a new penny after he washed them.

6

About three dozen round dark warriors' faces glared at the big bearded white man who rode boldly into their camp, as if he were leading a circus parade on this pleasantly cool summer afternoon.

Clutching bows, lances, and a couple of old muzzle-loading trade guns, the warriors lurked amid three rows of tepees that formed a ring around a central clearing. Inside the clearing, women scraped hides, ground corn, and braided hair ropes, while children scampered about.

The magnificent pinto inspired thoughts of theft among the warriors. Those notions were quickly dismissed, however, when they noticed that attached to the high cantle of Fargo's saddle was a six-foot-long pole that rose above his broad-brimmed hat. Like a ladder of banners, a string of fresh bloody scalps waved from the stick.

Fargo was doing his best to put on a show of audacity, and he hoped he was managing to hide the edginess he felt inside. Perhaps it was because the Indians were such good hunters that they began to think like their quarry: wild animals could sense fear in a man, and it often seemed that Indians were the same way. So Fargo acted as though he wasn't a bit worried about the Utes, even if that wasn't exactly the truth.

The Trailsman remained in the saddle as he reined up, yards from two old women and half a dozen girls, all busy at their metates, grinding corn and pretending that they weren't at all perturbed, either. Three of the girls were much too fair-skinned and thin-faced to be Utes. Several women working elsewhere in the camp looked Arapaho, while others still wore Hopi garb. That wasn't any surprise. The Utes trafficked in anything they could steal, whether that was pelts, horseflesh, or humans.

As Fargo sat stolidly, his lake-blue eyes flitting around the camp, the waiting game began. Turning his head to see what was happening behind him would be a sign of mistrust and weakness, so he watched those before him all the more closely. Any sudden shifts in their visages would turn him from a proud man into a fighting man.

Ignacio, chief of the Weeminuche band, eventually stepped out of a lodge. His clothes were a mixture of whatever he could steal that seemed impressive or comfortable. Most of today's delay might have been occasioned by the chief's need to dress in a way that would impress a white visitor; Fargo was under no illusions that his arrival was any kind of surprise.

Above his long braids, decorated with otter pelts, Ignacio wore a silk stovepipe hat with one eagle feather protruding from its rear. His faded blue coat had once been issued to a calvary trooper. The twill trousers might have come from any general store, except that the crotch had been cut out of them to allow for some deerhide breechings. He had on elaborate beaded moccasins with leggings that came almost to his knees.

The chief's high cheekbones got even higher when he smiled at the Trailsman. "If you are my brother and you come in peace, you will stand on the ground with me and we will smoke the pipe of friendship and talk like brothers. If you are my enemy, you will stay in your saddle and you will die there. I will put your scalp on top of that pole, and it will decorate my lodge, for I am a strong warrior."

"I am also a strong warrior with many scalps,"

Fargo replied, measuring his words carefully as his hand rested very close to the butt of his Colt. "Does Ignacio the leader of the Nuche believe that this is a good day to die?"

"Ignacio is not like Ouray the Arrow, whose heart is good but who is foolish and believed that the white eyes have good hearts too. A white eyes with a good heart would stand on the ground with me."

Fargo shook the scalp pole before replying. "Some of these are the scalps of men of your band." He released the pole. "My heart is not good," he confessed. "My heart is filled with hatred and sadness—"

Ignacio interrupted with a series of loud guffaws. He started laughing so hard that he ran out of breath. Finally the chief was able to talk. "You say your heart is not good. You are the first one my people have ever met."

"The first what?"

"The first white eyes who is honest and speaks the truth. The first white eyes who has the courage to say that his heart is not good. Come, stranger. My lodge is your lodge, my people's food is your food, our women are your women."

Fargo had borrowed some of the quartermaster's sweet-smelling tobacco, which he passed to Ignacio, who in turn passed it to a medicine man for a blessing before it was lit in the silver-ringed bowl of a yard-long ceremonial pipe. It was passed around while they squatted in Ignacio's lodge, and after an eternity of silence, Ignacio spoke.

"Why does this strange, truth-telling white eyes come to our camp with the bloody scalps of our men? Who is this white eyes?"

"I am called Skye Fargo by some. Others call me the Trailsman."

A pause followed. Among Utes, it was considered impolite to speak quickly after another man had spoken. You were supposed to take some time to think about what he had said. Otherwise, you weren't paying proper respect.

A young brave who looked at least half Apache broke the silence. "There are stories of the Trailsman. His medicine is strong, if the stories are true. He is not a man to have as an enemy, they say. Are you in war paint today, Trailsman? If you were a True Person, I would know your ways and I would know if you believed whether today was a good day to die. But you are not a True Person, so tell us."

Fargo eased back against a buffalo-hide backrest, took another puff on the pipe before passing it on, and thought about his reply.

"I did not wish to kill your brothers last night. But they were trying to steal our mules and horses. They would have killed me if I did not kill them first. I came to ask why your people would do such a thing when they have never done that before."

Ignacio grunted. "From the beginning of time when Coyote the Trickster opened the bag of Sinawaf, our people have taken what they have found. You do not know our ways if you say we have never done such things before."

The pipe came around again. "But the Horse Utes have never before bothered the surveyors who travel to the West so that they might know the land that their children ride upon."

"Surveyors? Men who look at rocks while running?" Ignacio's broad face looked worried.

Fargo nodded, then, after a proper interval, said, "Yes, a survey party. They are not settlers or prospectors. They are not here to take your land, only to measure it. The Nuche have always respected the surveyors and the surveyors have respected the Nuche. We do not steal from you and you do not steal from us."

"But you did not first come to our camp to smoke the pipe of peace and deliver presents to show your respect," the medicine man pointed out.

"That is because the True Persons did not leave a path to their camp that I could follow. As everyone knows, the True Persons are the best at following a trail, and they are also the best at hiding one." Though most white men would have gotten desperately lost on this morning's errand, Fargo had experienced no particular difficulty in finding the Ute camp. But a little flattery never hurt.

Ignacio beamed at the compliment, but then looked pained. "My warriors attacked a survey party? That is not what we were told that was."

This tedious, roundabout conversation was finally getting somewhere. "Ride with me to my camp and I will show you the rods and chains of the men who measure the ground. Your own strong eyes may stare through the looking tubes that bring far things close."

"My people were not told that. They were told that you were coming to plant your lodges upon our soil, scare away the deer and elk that my people eat, cut down the trees, rip the yellow metal from the sacred earth, and make the clear streams run bitter. That is what we were told, Trailsman, and that is why I allowed my braves to join with the red-haired man of your band to steal your stock and drive you away from the home of the True Persons. To measure the land and to draw pictures of it seems foolish to me, for the land goes as far as it goes and no one can know it from a picture. But it is true that the Nuche do not bother the surveyors. They are fools, but they are harmless fools."

Fargo fought his polite impulse to rise when a toothless, gray-haired old woman stepped into the tepee, bearing a steaming kettle, which she placed in the center of the ring of men. He just ignored her, as the Utes did, and felt glad that the pot contained fresh venison instead of rancid horse meat.

"If I had been the great leader of the Nuche and I had been told such things, I too would have joined the raid, and I would have taken many scalps and ponies,"

Fargo consoled, needling the chief about his failure to ride with his own warriors.

Ignacio looked a bit shamefaced about that. "I did not ride because my warriors were sure they could do it all by themselves. Young men are like that. They must prove that they are brave."

"You speak the truth. Young men of my tribe, too, can be headstrong from time to time. They do not listen to their elders." Now, to get this rambling conversation back to something the Trailsman wanted to know, without being too obvious about it. "It must have been a great liar who told you that we were not surveyors."

But despite Fargo's efforts, the conversation drifted to a recent battle with the Arapaho, up in South Park. Then the Utes laughed about some captives they had recently traded for tobacco and geegaws at the annual Taos fair. As the shadows grew long outside, they speculated as to how their ponies, mostly stolen, might fare in a race against the Ovaro.

The Utes didn't like to use torture, but Fargo's cramped thighs hadn't heard about this. His muscles were starting to burn, so he stood and stretched, apologizing to Ignacio.

"Do not tell me that my brother the Trailsman is tired of our company."

Fargo was more than tired of their company. But even if his visit hadn't been educational, this effort might avert a running war between the Utes and the survey party. So he told a polite lie—at least he hoped it was a lie—about how his band would get hopelessly lost if he were not there to scout for them.

"If you were truly my brother," Ignacio intoned, "you would stay here among your friends after the sun sets. Then you would ride to camp tomorrow, and you would know the things you came to learn from the True Persons."

Damn! Ignacio had caught on to what the Trailsman wanted to know: who was it that had put a few Utes up to last night's raid on the survey party? The wily chief wasn't going to pass the information on unless Fargo stayed the night and gave the Indians a chance to be hospitable—or to brain him in his sleep. Unconsciously, Fargo placed his hand on his revolver butt as he stood in the tepee door, thinking this through.

"If you truly believed you were among friends who mean you no harm, you would not stand there, ready to draw your pistol. You would instead lay down your gun."

Fargo wasn't about to unbuckle his gun belt. "I know that I am among friends. But I was also among friends last night, when my band was attacked in the darkness. I certainly needed my gun then. If the camp of the True Persons were attacked tonight, I would want to help you defend your women and children, the helpless ones. Do you wish to deny me the honor of helping you if you have the bad fortune to be attacked while I share your lodges?"

Ignacio seemed caught by that exercise in logic. He nodded. "My heart is glad that you stand ready to fight by our side."

Fargo stepped outside. Passing out a few chunks of hard candy made him the most popular man in camp. He found his Ovaro tethered to a long-needled ponderosa, munching grass placidly. One eager boy earned a whole sugar teat for showing Fargo where they had cached his gear, which looked in good order. That was somewhat surprising, considering how quickly things could disappear whenever there were Utes within reach. That scalp pole probably indicated some medicine that was too strong for youthful Utes to meddle with.

After a venison dinner, Fargo was directed to one of the smaller tepees. There his bedroll had been spread atop a soft carpet of buffalo hides that seemed alive with lice, ticks, and other hungry vermin. As far from his bedroll as was convenient, he laid a small chunk of warm venison he had filched from supper; the little pests just might decide to do their dining over there, instead of on him. He also pulled a small sulfur candle out of his saddlebag and lit it with a lucifer. The thing stank terribly, but its rank aroma would discourage the abundant flies, skeeters, gnats, bees, and wasps.

Feeling reasonably safe from an insect invasion, Fargo crawled into his bedroll, his Colt within easy reach as he got as comfortable as he could. Damn the Utes and their meandering ways of waiting around for half a week just to answer a simple question. Damn the Spanish for enslaving Indians and grabbing gold somewhere up here and starting three centuries of warfare. Damn the Americans for being so greedy that they'd kill for gold, even for a map nobody could read that might lead to some of that gold. Damn the government for insisting that every last chunk of the West had to be surveyed and mapped, so that someday people would be able to travel without hiring guides, leaving the Trailsman out of work. Damn the bastards, whoever they were, who were trying to stop the survey, whatever their reasons were.

And damn the day this smelly, sulfur candle was fluttering, which meant somebody was messing with the flaps. Fargo got his hand on his pistol and decided he could fire it through the blankets if necessary.

Old Indian women weren't nearly as harmless as they looked. In many tribes, the old women were in charge of torturing prisoners. That might not be the case here, but there was absolutely no reason on earth to trust the aged crone who crept through the flap, then straightened and stared at the Trailsman.

His eyes mere slits, Fargo stared back. It was painful to examine this woman, who had to be one of Ignacio's wives. The yellow cast of the candle gave her drooping, wrinkled arms a jaundiced tint. Her gray hair was braided, but odd stalks stuck out at bizarre angles. She looked like the same woman who had brought in the stew earlier today; her lined face had the same puffy eyelids and toothless mouth.

Mercifully, her face disappeared, but that was only

because she was pulling up the tattered doeskin dress that had covered up most of her body. Fargo fought the temptation to wince when he saw the drooping breasts beneath that sagged almost to her puffy waist. He let his eyes close before he saw anything more. Just hearing her cackle as she eyed him was bad enough.

Fargo recalled Ignacio's speech, about how the Ute lodge was the guest's lodge and the Ute women were the Trailsman's women. Damn. Once you accepted those offers by agreeing to stay, you were along for the ride, wherever it took you.

He sure couldn't tell this hag that he wasn't interested in what she had to offer. Not without angering the entire band here. He might manage to escape tonight after such an insult, but this band would get surly at the affront to their hospitality. Then weeks of running warfare between the survey party and the local Utes would follow, with triple night guards on the horses, which still wouldn't keep some from being stolen, and any whites who got caught alone would be killed and scalped.

Feigning sleep might work, but he'd have to be so good at it that a probing woman wouldn't notice. Fargo doubted he was that good an actor.

But how the hell good an actor would a man have to be to pleasure this homely woman? Just the thought of her made him shrivel. It wasn't fair. An unattractive old woman probably wanted the same things from a man that any other woman did. But there were limits to what a man could do, and Fargo felt like that limit, as far as this woman was concerned, had been passed about twenty years and thirty pounds ago.

Maybe if he kept his eyes closed tightly, didn't move his hands across that leathery flesh, and just imagined, imagined with every nerve he had, that he was with a saucy Arapaho girl, then maybe he'd get through the night without starting a war.

Fargo let his eyes drift open again. She sat on his bedroll beside him, staring at his full beard. That profuse growth must have been a novelty to her, for most Ute men could barely grow mustaches.

The Trailsman decided that he might as well get this over with, and forced himself to smile. The woman looked annoyed at first, then smiled back. She rubbed her wind-chapped cheeks with her hands. A disgusted look crept across her as she rubbed a hand against Fargo's hairy cheek. She made motions like the opening and stropping of a razor. The edge of her palm made chopping motions across Fargo's chin.

Fargo frowned to hide his inner elation. They agreed on something. He didn't see her as desirable, and she thought he was as ugly as a man could get, on account of his beard. He shook his head to indicate that he wasn't about to shave, just to please her. He sat up and used sign language to stretch the truth a bit, as he explained that among his people, a beard was the mark of a great warrior. Even though he wanted to make the Ute woman happy, he must keep that disgusting hair on his face, or he would be shamed when he returned to his band.

Her quick gestures showed that she understood. Even better, she stood and pulled that dress over her. At the entry flap, she signed a message that she hoped that he would not hold it against the True Persons that their best women did not find him appealing. Fargo replied that he knew the True Persons had good hearts and that he was not insulted by the strange preferences of their womenfolk. He added that he was tired and he wanted to fall asleep.

He thought she understood that, but he awoke to a spluttering candle. For a moment or two, he feared that some flying insects had developed a taste for sulfur fumes and were rustling about his beard, looking for tender places to dine on. But when he shifted, he realized that his beard was being disturbed by a woman's soft hand.

"*¿Habla español?*" she wondered when she saw that he was somewhat awake. Although dressed in Ute garb and sporting long dark braids, she obviously wasn't even a distant relative. Her thin nose and almost hollow cheeks, as well as her mellifluous Spanish, were traits of an hidalgo woman. Perhaps she had been captured by Comanche, then traded to Utes, who might again trade her the next time the band wandered to the market at Taos.

"No," Fargo sighed. He spoke enough border Mexican to get by when he had to, but telling her that he spoke Spanish would have been stretching matters farther than necessary. *"¿Hable inglés?"* he queried.

"Sí." She smiled, then blushed. "Yes. Though not good." Her hand continued to caress the Trailsman's beard. "That is the mark of a true man," she sighed. Her free hand grasped Fargo's right hand and pressed it against her chest.

The shapeless smock, made of calico trade cloth, concealed a marvelous pair of round breasts, soft but firm, that Fargo's hand eagerly massaged, paying special attention to the ripe nipples that grew ever riper during his exploration. His other hand found a bare knee near his neck, and her silken thigh felt as good as the rest of her.

Though she was cooperative, she wasn't in any hurry to shed her dress. Removing it took the better part of a pleasant half an hour of probing, kissing, and fondling.

By then, she was as ready as the Trailsman, and he'd never felt more eager in his life. He twisted their tangled embrace so that she was on bottom, and he plunged deeply in as her lithe thighs gained a scissors lock on his torso.

"Oh, my God," she gasped as her moist flesh arched up against Fargo's insistent loins. "You are too much for me."

But he knew that was just flattery, and he pressed home deeper, moving slowly but steadily as the sensitive tip of his blood-gorged shaft found a haven.

"No, no, no more," she cried, but when Fargo eased his probing, she blinked her long dark eyelashes and urged him onward. "More, more, *muy, muy, macho*." Every time she changed her mind, her voice got louder. Fargo hoped they weren't entertaining the night sentries at this camp, but he really didn't care. All he cared about was this woman beneath him who now had her legs locked behind him.

Somehow she rolled back so that only her head and shoulders lay on anything solid. Her expansive breasts vibrated, jutting into the reach of his flickering tongue. The rest of her soared upward, seemingly suspended by his thrusting shaft.

"Now, now, now," she insisted.

Fargo felt the pressure build as her moans became gasps that became screams that he had to smother with his own lips. But when he bent low to cover her mouth with his, she pulled in his tongue, just as she wanted to pull in the rest of him. Rather than smothering her sound, he intensified it. He thrust hard, and she threw her head back and screeched like a riled mountain lion.

Her internal muscles began to grip, to massage him as she pushed her dripping cleft against his solid flesh and rotated savagely. Her hands rose to cup his cheeks. She buried her grasping fingers in his full beard. She laughed with great spasms whenever he brushed low and tickled her sensitive nipples.

"Now, now. Do not make me wait."

Just on the off chance that her latest tumultuous shout had not wakened the entire camp, Fargo obliged her, exploding with a surge that made every muscle of his body quiver. If there were any parts of her that didn't respond the same way, he sure didn't notice them. A long wail of satisfaction soared from her glistening lips as she pulled his head down, eager for him to silence her with an extended, gasping kiss that continued until they both were exhausted.

When morning came, all too early, she was still at Fargo's side, every limb wrapped around him.

Once he got himself assembled and outside, Ignacio

met him with a knowing smile. "Do you wish to buy her, Trailsman? She is not an easy wife for me."

Fargo looked at the chief's rotund and hairless face. He seemed serious about bargaining, and the woman was obviously a captive who belonged somewhere else. This might be her only chance of escape for some time. "She is worth much, but I have little to pay with," he replied after a polite interval.

"To me she is worth little. One horse?"

"I travel with only one. I cannot spare him."

Buying the captive hidalgo woman who didn't like men who didn't have beards would please the local Utes, which would greatly simplify his work with the surveyors. And besides that, there were still some things that Fargo wanted to know about the raid the other night. So he grabbed his saddlebags and pulled out a long rope of twisted tobacco. Then he grabbed a two-pound sack of hard candy and a bag of gaudy beads. Ignacio invited him into the chief's lodge, and Fargo got ready for some hard bargaining.

7

The flagpole and the nine long adobe barracks that formed Fort Garland were coming into sight in the vast valley at the west foot of Sangre de Cristo Pass.

Captain Macomber, riding abreast of the Trailsman, turned to his companion. "You're sure we won't have any more Indian trouble now." He sounded rather dubious.

"I didn't say that," Fargo reminded. "What I did say was that I'd be willing to bet a large sum that we won't have any more trouble with that particular band of Utes."

"What's that supposed to mean?" Macomber reined his huge gray mule to a slow walk.

"Ignacio is the chief of the Weeminuche Utes, and he understands that we're just surveyors that don't mean any harm to him and his band. They'll leave us alone. But his word doesn't mean a thing to any Kiowas, Comanche, Cheyenne, Arapaho, or Jicarilla Apache who might be roaming hereabouts."

Macomber nodded. "I guess that's understandable. But this is pretty much Ute territory, isn't it?"

Fargo chuckled. "The Utes sure wish everybody thought that way. But keep in mind that Ignacio is chief of just his own band. There are other bands of Utes that frequent this valley from time to time, like the Muache, Capote, Tabeguache, and Uncompahgre."

"So just because we're on good terms with Ignacio's

band of Weeminuches doesn't mean we can count on getting along with the others," the captain complained, a glum note creeping into his voice.

"Well, it sure won't hurt," Fargo consoled. "And we'll have some soldiers from Garland to help us if we get in a fight."

Macomber's voice got even glummer. "Don't count on that. Colonel Canby called most of the regulars of the Tenth Infantry down to Santa Fe and Albuquerque because he needed men there. From what I heard through the army grapevine, there are only a couple of regular army officers and noncoms at Garland."

Fargo gazed out at the fort, only a mile away. By now, any army post run in a halfway organized manner would have sent some riders out to see who was approaching. Or else, his party would have run into some outlying sentries. "So who is running the fort?"

"There's a regiment of two hundred men. They're local volunteers, sort of like a militia. I'm sure they mean well, but I don't know how much good they'd be if we got in a jam. And I don't know if they could spare any troops for protection if we should need some while we're running the survey to the north."

Shit. Fargo had hoped that some soldiers would be available so he could take off a couple days to run an important errand: returning a captive woman to her family.

From what Fargo had been able to piece together, Consuelo Gallegos had family down near Santa Fe. She understandably wanted to return to them. Out on the Cimarron Cutoff early this summer, Comanches had abducted her from a caravan when she had been returning to Santa Fe from school in St. Louis. They had traded her to some Utes, who had apparently planned on taking her to the annual fair at Taos, and either selling her or collecting a ransom from her family.

But the Utes hadn't driven a real hard bargain for her. Ignacio went through the usual song and dance during the trade, but his heart didn't seem to be in it. Consuelo might not have been all that good at grinding corn, scraping hides, or setting up tepees, but when she crawled under the blankets after sundown, she more than made up for those deficiencies. Yet Ignacio had settled for six feet of rope tobacco, a few dozen beads, a bag of candy, and a couple small iron loops that sparked when you struck them against a chunk of flint. And Fargo had the feeling that if he'd held out a little longer, the chief would have just given her away.

That wasn't the only troubling thing about her. Some Spanish gentry didn't think it was worth the trouble to teach their girls to read and write at all. Others had duennas who taught those skills, or else the girls were sent to convents for a year or two. But Fargo had never heard of any hidalgo family sending a girl to school in the East. And when the taciturn woman spoke, which was seldom, he didn't get the idea that she was all that educated, anyway.

She definitely wasn't a Ute, though, so Fargo decided he had done the right thing.

As if he could read the Trailsman's thoughts, Macomber broke in. "What are you going to do with the woman? You know my policy on that."

Fargo nodded sullenly. Macomber had been angry when the Trailsman returned from the Ute camp with Consuelo riding double. In the captain's view, having a woman around camp would cause morale problems. Men whose minds should be on their work would begin to think about other things. Men would be showing off for her, which would lead to fights and dissension. Fargo understood the captain's concerns, even if he enjoyed having someone so warm and willing to share his bedroll at night.

"I'm hoping that the commanding officer will give me a couple days off so I can take her down to the town of San Luis."

As a sentry finally hailed them, only a hundred

yards from the fort, Macomber looked relieved. "San Luis? That's very near. I thought, though, that you said her family was in Santa Fe."

"That's what she told me," Fargo explained. "But Santa Fe is a four-day ride, and San Luis is close by. There are a lot of people named Gallegos in San Luis, so there's a good chance that she might have some uncles or cousins nearby who will take care of her. And if that doesn't work out, I know a few people down there who might help her out."

After assuring the out-of-uniform sentry that he had no plans to plunder Fort Garland, Macomber answered Fargo. "We'll be at the fort a day or two before we start running lines to the north. So I don't see any problem with giving you a short leave, Fargo. Just get back as soon as you can. When are you taking off?"

Fargo glanced up at the sun, high and brilliant in the azure sky. The only clouds in sight were far to the west, looming over the San Juan Mountains, which formed one wall of this huge valley, sixty miles away from the Sangre de Cristos they had just crossed.

"Now's about as good a time as any," Fargo replied. It galled him to have to explain where he was going and when he planned to return, although he understood why Macomber wanted to know. "Should be able to get down there before dark, and I can come back in the morning, if all goes well. Tomorrow night at the latest."

"Vaya con Dios!" Macomber waved. The captain rode forward to talk to the post commander.

Fargo turned back to the rest of the pack train, found Consuelo flirting amid a group of surveyors and their assistants, and told her it was time to go home.

Since the main supply route for Fort Garland came up from the south, the road that way was fairly wide and smooth. It twisted along the east flank of the jagged Sangre de Cristos. The road sat above the bottomlands, thus preserving the fields and avoiding the deepest of the springtime mud, but it generally wound around the talons of the mountains, instead of climbing over each buttressing ridge, and thus stayed reasonably level.

It was the kind of wagon road a thoughtful surveyor would lay out, and Fargo momentarily wondered what had come over him—here he was thinking about laying out roads when he was riding with an attractive woman.

But Consuelo wasn't very talkative, nor did she appear at all interested in the countryside. She just sat, as demurely as a woman could who wasn't aboard a proper sidesaddle, atop her government mule. A borrowed broad-brimmed felt hat shaded her thin face. Her chestnut hair was pinned up under the hat, and the rest of her was pretty much covered by an oversized canvas duster one of the survey crew had lent her.

As the road dipped for the easy fording of placid Ojito Creek, only a couple yards wide and barely running at all this late in the summer, Fargo felt Consuelo's dark eyes fixed upon him. He met her gaze with a question. "Is something wrong?"

"Everything," she hissed.

"How's that? It's a nice day in good country and you're on your way home after being an Indian captive."

"But how can I face them?" Her black mule halted at the edge of the creek, unwilling to proceed unless prodded. Consuelo seemed more intent on prodding the Trailsman. "What they must think of me. I have been shamed."

"It wasn't your doing," Fargo consoled. "Most folks who have any choice at all in the matter don't get carried off by Comanche."

She started to say something, then clenched her lips and blushed. "But I am not presentable. How is one to bathe amid all those soldiers?"

Hardly any of the men in their party had been soldiers, but Fargo saw her point. "This is probably the only water we'll cross before the Río Seco, and that's right on the edge of town. So if you want to stop here and freshen up, I think I can find something else to do for a few minutes."

He dismounted and helped her alight, then pointed to a willow-lined pool that started a few yards downstream. Once she got past the tree-shaded bend, she'd have all the privacy she might want. Making of lot of noise as the branches gave way, Consuelo stepped toward the pool while Fargo loosened the cinches to give his Ovaro and the mule a break as they drank their fill. Then he hobbled them and got comfortable beneath a cottonwood.

Fargo's lazy reverie was disturbed a few minutes later when he heard splashing close by. Springing to his feet and grabbing his Colt, he spun, peering downstream.

From behind some overhanging greenery, Consuelo appeared, knee-deep in the water and glistening all over. Her breasts heaved delightfully as she invited him to join her. "Surely you, too, wish to be clean before you enter a town?" she encouraged.

What Fargo suddenly had in mind wasn't going to make him a bit cleaner, except perhaps as a side effect, but he didn't waste any time in returning his Colt to its holster. "You're sure you want to do this?" he wondered.

At her enthusiastic nod, Fargo walked over to the pool and left a pile of clothes on the rockiest part of its bank before stepping in. He actually did manage to wash off some trail dust and sweat before Consuelo arrived with a dewy and encompassing embrace.

Her cool hand found his swelling shaft and began to stroke, slowly with a passionate grasp. "We must make sure that part of you is clean."

Fargo had no objection. His hands started at her shoulders and slid slowly down, kneading her smooth flesh. His eager hands came forward to cup her breasts, the erect nipples hard and almost cold against his callused fingers as well as his softer palms.

While a sighing and moaning Consuelo continued to

caress his throbbing erection, he kept one hand at a breast and rubbed her back with the other—down to the small, then the swell of her firm buttocks, which fit comfortably in his palm. He rotated and massaged, though it became more difficult. She kept arching her rump back while bending her torso lower, and soon her forehead was pressing against him, just above his navel.

Her head slid down just a bit, wet hair tickling his belly. A smooth wetness flicked at the sensitive tip of his pole, followed by a long exploration by the rest of her insistent tongue. It felt so good that Fargo shook a bit with the excitation.

Those dark eyes with fluttering lashes looked up at him. "Does this bother you? Do you want me to stop?"

Fargo hoped she could see his broad smile. "Whatever suits you will suit me."

Consuelo began to purr like a satisfied cat, though it was obvious that she wasn't anywhere near satisfied with just a few licks. After her tongue explored every throbbing vein, she moved back a few inches and knelt; the shallow water almost reached her narrow waist. Those thin lips formed a circle at the nib of his shaft. Slowly her head moved forward, engulfing the swollen and pulsing tip. She held it there for a moment, swirling her tongue to provide pleasures that he had only imagined.

Fargo was of two minds. He wanted to watch her performance, and he also wanted to rock his head back toward the darkening afternoon sky and shout his ecstasy to the heavens.

He did a little of both as her amazing progress continued. Wet hair brushing her shoulders, Consuelo's head bobbed back and forth as she sucked like a hungry calf, her whole body quivering with anticipation, just as Fargo's was. Standing there anxious and weak-kneed, he could feel every particle of the hot breath from that turned-up nose, every tiny roughness on that exquisite and inspired tongue, every bit of ecstatic smooth pressure that her lips and mouth could provide.

His shuddering explosion came with such force that he was surprised when he looked down and saw that she was not across the pool, but still kneeling before him with a dreamy look as she licked her lips. She sighed and smiled as Fargo patted her head, not sure what else to do.

Finally she spoke. "You are a man who can truly enjoy many pleasures, I see. So many men, when someone wishes to love them . . ."

Fargo shook his head and raised a finger to his lips. "What other folks do isn't our worry, is it? All that's important is what we do with each other."

At her nod, Fargo suggested that if they'd lay a blanket on the bank, she might be more comfortable. He'd enjoy feeling her silken thighs pressed against his ears while he returned some of her favors. As usual, he was glad to oblige a lady. Fargo decided to spend the night camped nearby.

When he awoke, early the next morning, sun burning at his face, Consuelo was gone. Fargo cursed himself for getting so exhausted and spent, then he found her over by the horses. In attempting to help get things ready, she must have gotten tangled up in the ropes and bridles. Both her wrists and one forearm had nasty rope burns on them, which he salved.

Two hours later, they rode into San Luis, the tiny settlement that had given its name to the huge valley that sprawled to the north and west. You really couldn't see much of that valley from San Luis because it sat under a piñon-clad butte. A field of corn and beans, irrigated by a community ditch, extended for about a mile eastward, to where farming was impossible on account of the mountains rising there.

The town itself wasn't much more than a few log jacales and small adobe buildings at the perimeter of its plaza. Off to the side, just under the mesa, was the town's main industry, a mill where grindstones turned out flour. At the plaza there was a market, a cantina, a livery stable, and a smithy. The other buildings held families. Unlike Yankee farmers, who lived on their farms, these men lived in town and walked out every morning to till their fields.

There wasn't anyone in town now, however. If it had been noontime, then the daily siesta during the hot hours would explain that. But this was early in the day.

Fargo reined the Ovaro to a halt and thought for a moment. Although it was only a decade old, San Luis was the oldest town in Colorado Territory. Several families of colonists from New Mexico had founded the settlement back in 1851, but that hadn't been their first try: Previous efforts had been driven out by rampaging Indians. Had something made the settlers flee? He looked around. No Indian sign, no burned-out buildings or the like. The water wheel turned at the mill, and there were a few horses in the corral by the livery.

With Consuelo at his side, Fargo went to the stable, where he found several men lounging inside. Although he knew a few people in San Luis—he passed through here from time to time, since it lay on the main road north of Taos—none of his acquaintances were among these men. They glared at him with open suspicion that could turn into outright hostility at any moment. He gave the usual greetings, which were answered with sullen grunts.

"Is Darío Gallegos still the alcalde here?" Fargo decided it was time to find out where everyone was, and the name of the storekeeper, who also served as a mayor of a sort, seemed like a good place to start.

Several men nodded. After a tense moment, the youngest of them tightened a grip on his pistol as he spoke up. "Why do you wish to know, gringo?"

"Isn't it your custom for strangers in town to state their business to the alcalde? I will be happy to speak to him, but I see no reason to discuss my business with strangers." Fargo punctuated this with an icy glare and a swing of his hand down to the butt of his Colt.

One of the other men decided to insult Fargo by addressing Consuelo without first asking his permission. "*Señorita,* how may we help you?"

Consuelo stepped away from Fargo and toward him. "By taking me away from this filthy beast," she hissed.

Surprised as hell, considering how friendly they'd just been, Fargo stepped back. Consuelo held up her hands, letting the duster's sleeves drop so that the fresh, self-inflicted rope burns on her wrists showed. "This big pig, he captured me and bound me," she wailed. "He abused me."

Eager to defend a woman's honor, the men began to draw their pistols. Fargo's first hurried round tore the gun out of the youngest man's hand, smashing a couple of fingers in the process, as blood spurted up and fell like crimson raindrops to the dank dirt floor.

Before the first drops hit, the Trailsman edged sideways, toward the door. He didn't really want to kill anybody in here, but this wasn't the time for talking. As a bullet thudded into the adobe wall, sending up a cloud of dust that sprayed against his ear, he poked a bullet into a serape-clad shoulder. The short husky man spun, spoiling the aim of the man next to him. Consuelo was scatting out the back door as Fargo sidled through the front, racing toward the market as the door stopped three bullets.

Consuelo was running toward some cottonwoods that shaded the far end of town, but Fargo didn't care what happened to her at the moment. He needed to find Darío Gallegos, the alcalde, and get things settled before a full-blown war erupted here.

Gallegos came out of the store, but halted at Fargo's shout. "Let's go inside and talk."

The alcalde nodded, but then grew puzzled when behind Fargo, four men—two of them bleeding, but all of them angry and toting guns—came roaring out of the livery. Fargo flattened as the first shots came, but those sailed harmlessly overhead, and by then, the local leader had managed to calm his citizens. They agreed to meet at the cantina, where Fargo could explain why he'd been abusing one of their women.

Once seated across the table from Gallegos, while other men of San Luis crowded the room, Fargo wasn't too sure what to say. It would be his word against Consuelo's, and he didn't have a bit of doubt whom they would believe. But maybe he had a chance, since Consuelo seemed to have vanished among the trees. At his urging, Gallegos told three men to go look for her and bring her in.

Then the bearded storekeeper smiled. "Please accept my most sincere and heartfelt apologies, Fargo, for your rude welcome. I am sure that there must be a misunderstanding. For as long as I have been here, you have always been my friend and you have always kept your word. I shall never forget how you retrieved my sheep from those Utes two years ago. Nor can the people of San Luis ever repay the debt we owe you for killing those thieves who preyed upon our wagons between here and Fernández de Taos."

At this bit of history concerning several of the Trailsman's passages through here, the six men remaining in the room quieted and stopped glaring so hard. Fargo nodded and decided it was best for Gallegos to do the talking.

"Now, Fargo, I know that you do not wish any ill to the people of my village. And if you care to tell us, I should like to hear why you have come to us."

Even if Gallegos had made it sound otherwise, Fargo didn't have any choice except to explain. He started by mentioning the survey party up north that he was supposed to be serving as the scout for, providing he ever got back.

At his mention of the survey, one of the men at the closest table starting shouting in rapid-fire Spanish. Fargo couldn't make out the words, but he got the impression that the man wasn't praising the surveyors.

"Is what my neighbor says the truth, Fargo?" Gallegos had a sad stare as he poured down a tiny glass of fiery mescal.

"I'm sorry," Fargo apologized, "but he spoke too quickly. I can't tell you whether what he said is true or not until I know what he said."

Gallegos translated.

Fargo slumped back, relieved on this account. "Darío, please explain this to your village. Despite what people at the livery stable were told by a mysterious rider that passed through yesterday, the surveyors are not out to take anyone's land away. All they're doing is mapping a few roads and setting the boundaries of some land grants north of Fort Garland."

Gallegos passed that on, but the men still looked dubious, so Fargo continued. "Your boundaries here were settled long ago, by the New Mexico Territorial surveyor, before there was a Colorado. You know that the surveyor didn't take your property then. You still have your fields and your commons and your town. I know that you and your people often have reasons to suspect that Uncle Sam is trying to steal your land with these surveys, but that is not what's going on now. If there were any plans to steal your houses and your fields, to open your property to other settlers, then I give you my solemn word that I would then be fighting at your side."

Fargo became just about as popular as he had been unpopular. After several cheers, and some apologetic handshakes, he was almost comfortable. They would, however, still have some questions about Consuelo, and he had some questions about this rumor-monger they had heard from yesterday. Somebody was trying to stop the survey. Whoever it was had stirred up the Utes, and when that hadn't worked, he had come through and tried to rile up the settlers here. Fargo would bet money that similar rumors were circulating in the nearby hamlets of San Pedro and San Francisco.

While he still had friends here, the Trailsman covered some of his story with Consuelo, how she was from Santa Fe and the Comanche had taken her and sold her to the Utes, and how he had traded her away from the Utes, with reasonably pure intentions of returning her to her family.

That didn't explain the rope burns, but the alcalde wasn't concerned about them.

"Fargo, I am a Gallegos."

Fargo nodded, since there didn't seem to be anything he could say to that.

"I do not travel much, but people pass through here often. I stay current on the news of my family. And I can assure you that there never was such a woman in the Gallegos family. I would certainly have heard if a woman from our family had gone to school in St. Louis, for such a thing is most unusual. And I would have heard if a Gallegos had been taken captive by the Indians, for such matters are talked of widely. I have not heard of such things. I have not seen this woman you have all spoken of, but I am willing to swear that her true name cannot be Consuelo Gallegos. Fargo, the men of our village were misled by a passing man. I fear that you have been misled by a woman."

There were a few muted laughs, which Fargo felt like joining. Not because he thought it was all that funny to get taken in like that, but because he finally felt at ease here.

Maybe the woman was part of the effort to stop the survey. She was open-minded about a lot of things, so she certainly could have arranged to travel with the Utes, who would accept just about anybody who was willing to put up with them. Chief Ignacio had been in a hurry to get rid of her, and it was warriors from his band that had launched an attack on the survey crew.

But if it was a conspiracy to stop the survey, who was behind it? And why? Fargo took another shot of mescal, which would either make him think faster or stop thinking at all. The answers usually came when you figured out who had something to gain. Which brought thoughts of that old parchment map in his saddlebags. If it indeed led to a cache of Spanish treasure, then there was enough profit to inspire all sorts of trouble.

Fargo lifted his glass to Gallegos and asked the storekeeper if he could get rid of the others so that they might talk in private. If anybody would know what was going on around here, Darío Gallegos should.

8

With a shake of his steel-gray hair, a commanding expression on his hawklike visage, Darío Gallegos cleared the cantina and told one of his sons to go mind the store. He returned his attention to the Trailsman, who stood and stretched before returning to his seat across the battered wooden table.

"This is about as private as matters can get in San Luis." The storekeeper smiled.

"I know, San Luis is a little town where even the thickest adobe walls have ears, and nothing stays secret for more than an afternoon."

"Make that twenty minutes, and you would be more correct." Gallegos laughed. "But tell me, Fargo, how can I help you?"

"I need to know some local lore." The mescal had been replaced by a crockery jug of dry white wine. Fargo poured a glass and sipped at it, just to be polite. It was so acidic that he puckered. He hoped Gallegos was polite enough to ignore that inadvertent commentary on the local winery.

Gallegos chuckled and muttered, "It is an acquired taste." Then he raised his voice. "What sort of lore? There are many tales and legends, so many that you would be an old man long before you heard them all."

"Let's start with that land grant to the north of Garland," Fargo suggested. "Somehow, I think those people are connected to a lot of the trouble I've been running into."

"How so?"

Fargo chuckled. "You, too, would be a very old man before I finished telling you all of it. Basically, my problem is that somebody doesn't want this survey to happen. The survey concerns that land grant. So it stands to reason that there's a connection."

Gallegos leaned back, hands folded below the pointed tip of his gray-streaked beard. As Fargo's impatience built, the storekeeper mulled. Finally he opened his eyes, sipped from his glass, and began to explain.

"I was a young man who paid little mind to politics in 1845, when war broke out between the United States and Mexico, and the American soldiers conquered this region, mostly without ever firing a gun. So much of what I say is what I have heard, not what I know."

"Anything that concerns politics is usually that way," Fargo commented, his voice as dry as the wine.

"But consider the situation in those days. Arthur Ellsworth, a man of Massachusetts, ventured west in 1840. Just before the war, he obtained a land grant from Pedro Armijo, the Mexican governor."

"I thought those land grants were reserved for Mexican citizens." By the eighth or tenth sip, the wine began to taste tolerable to the Trailsman. So tolerable that he was starting to feel a bit light-headed.

"Those bequests of land were restricted to citizens," Gallegos confirmed. "So this man Ellsworth arranged matters through the Espinoza family, and was rewarded with the land you wanted to know of—the vast grant to the north of Fort Garland which had boundaries your people now want to survey. It was all in the Espinoza name, but everyone suspects that he was standing right behind them."

Fargo pondered that for a few moments. "I might have heard the name a time or two, but I can't say that I know anything at all about this Ellsworth fellow."

"He seldom visits this region. He remains in the East, while the Espinozas do all the work on the grant. There has been talk that he is attempting to sell it to a foreign syndicate—English or Dutch, I believe, though I am not sure. At any rate, they might have the capital to develop its fields and forests, to place sawmills and flour mills, to dig mines for the ores of the earth."

From the sad tone of the storekeeper's voice, Fargo got the impression that Gallegos didn't like that idea. But maybe it explained why there was such an effort coming from somewhere to stop the survey. Ellsworth, if he wanted to sell all fifty or sixty square miles, would need its boundaries defined precisely because no sensible buyer would touch the land otherwise.

Also, if the local residents didn't want the sale to go through, then they might think that stopping the survey would stop the sale. Life at the north end of the valley could still go on in its traditional informal way, where you herded your flocks and gathered your firewood just about anywhere you pleased, land grants or no. Once a profit-hungry foreign syndicate got hold of the land, however, the borders would be fenced and what had been the normal daily routine would become criminal trespassing.

But then again, Fargo hadn't seen much evidence that any of these settlers cared one way or another about stopping the survey. They had plenty else to keep themselves busy. Things might be different to the north, though. Damn. This was perplexing. Maybe it was time to think about something else, such as why some people were so murderously eager to get their hands on that map that nobody could understand.

"Darío, what are the stories of Spanish treasure hidden hereabouts?"

Gallegos refilled his glass and glanced around. Even though the room was empty, his voice still dropped to a conspiratorial tone. "Should you live a thousand years, Fargo, and do nothing but listen, you would never hear the end of such stories. I think it is because there is not much to do here during the winter, except to lie close with one's woman and, when one is not doing that, to go to the cantina and make up stories to tell others about great treasures hidden in these mountains. For my part, I believe the true treasures are those we make ourselves, our farms to feed us and our families."

Fargo stood and shrugged his massive shoulders, inhaling deeply to clear his head after the wine. "I suspect you're right. But is there any tale about a treasure that might be anywhere near that grant? A story that might come within a day's ride of being half-true?"

As Fargo returned to his chair, Gallegos sat with his dark eyes closed. "Only one," he announced when he opened them. "And it is fairly simple. It may well hold some truth, for I heard it from my grandparents, who were people who held the truth quite dear."

Back in 1779, the Spanish authorities in Madrid had put General Juan Bautista de Anza in charge of New Mexico. Unlike the usual run of political appointees who were in it solely for the graft and the bribes they could collect, de Anza had been an energetic and concerned leader.

Some Ute bands were then friendly with the Spanish. To the north of the territorial capital of Santa Fe, these Utes had pretty much settled down to farm a little and raise stock. Trouble was, the unsettled Comanche kept raiding their villages. The Utes appealed for help from the Spanish, and de Anza raised an army and marched north to punish the Comanche and recover Ute stock and captives.

They followed the tracks of the raiding Comanche, up into the San Luis Valley, and then over Poncha Pass to the Arkansas River, deep in the heart of the main range of the Rocky Mountains.

"De Anza turned east there, for that is where the Comanche appeared to have gone," Gallegos continued. "The general later defeated them and their chief—Cuerno Verde, or Green Horn in your language—in a great battle near the edge of the plains."

Fargo nodded. "I heard that much of the story once when I asked how Green Horn Peak got its name. Did the Comanche have some treasure? Doesn't sound likely to me."

"No," Gallegos explained. "As the story goes, six men of de Anza's army were to scout farther up the Arkansas, to see if the Comanche had ventured that way. Near its headwaters, high in the mountains, they found huge golden nuggets, and they deserted so that they could gather the gold and keep it to themselves."

There was still a large quantity of placer gold up at the top of the Arkansas, or else there wouldn't be a mining camp there now called Oro City. So this story was starting to make some sense, Fargo decided. He urged Gallegos to continue.

"After collecting three or four hundred pounds of gold, the soldiers did not know where to turn. As the story goes, one of them was Carlos Hernández, who had once been a priest before he was caught in the bed of a woman of his congregation. It was Hernández who suggested that they ride south, cache the gold somewhere, and reunite with de Anza's army. They could avoid the penalty for desertion—death after slow torture—by claiming that they were attacked by the savages. Then later they could return to their hidden gold."

"And where was this gold supposed to be hidden?"

"Who is to say?" Gallegos shrugged. "If I knew, I would go get it myself. But there is more to this tale, if you wish to hear it."

Fargo shook his head to fight off the drowsy feeling that came with the wine. "Go right ahead. I'm listening."

The Spanish army had swung round the narrow canyons of the Arkansas when it headed east. Then the pursuing soldiers went south, into the valley that was rimmed on the east by the rolling Wet Mountains and on the west by the jagged Sangre de Cristos. The deserting soldiers followed that route, about two weeks behind the army.

The big battle with the Comanches was over before they got there, but de Anza's army didn't destroy all the Comanche. There were still a few dozen roaming the area, and when they caught sight of six Spanish soldiers, a running battle began. At least one of the soldiers was killed as they retreated up the Sangre de Cristos. They were losing horses, too, and toting all that gold was getting to be an awful lot of work.

So somewhere near the crest of the Sangres, they found a deep cave and hid the gold, just before the Comanche arrived. Hernández was the only one to escape: He supposedly drew a map a year or two later, when he came down with a fever that killed him, shortly after he prepared the map for his son.

"That is the story, and if it is true, then that cave full of gold must lie close by the Espinoza grant, or perhaps, within the grant," Gallegos concluded. "But as I have said, there are many matters for a man to concern himself with which are more worth his time."

Fargo nodded in agreement. "I think you've got the right idea." Before he could continue, three dispirited men burst through the door.

The Trailsman wasn't too worried, since they were the same three that Gallegos had sent after Consuelo. The tallest of them had a report that sounded sad in Spanish, and Fargo understood why when Gallegos translated. Consuelo had vanished. They had followed her to the cottonwoods along the acequia—the irrigation canal—and then she wasn't there. A rider must have picked her up, but there were many tracks, too many of them to determine much more.

"You are the Trailsman, Fargo," Gallegos announced. "Surely you can read the ground and tell us what became of the woman."

Fargo nodded and rose. "I'll take a look. But I've got to be heading back to Garland shortly, or we'll have the whole army down here, looking for me."

But the army was already on its way. He could hear the pounding of hooves and the shouts of men as he stepped out into the plaza. Before he was done blinking to adjust to the sunshine, a blue-coated sergeant had already dismounted, and several dozen more men were pulling in.

"Get indoors, everybody," the husky sergeant with the dust-streaked blond beard ordered.

Fargo just stayed outdoors and, with Gallegos at his side, stepped closer to the sergeant. "What's going on?" Fargo asked.

The sergeant spun on his run-down heel and drew a saber, which kept Fargo at a respectful distance. "This town is now under martial law until we deal with the hostile uprising."

Fargo glanced around at the mounted troopers. They weren't really troopers. Aboard an assortment of mounts that ranged from calvary horses to long-eared Spanish burros, they were the volunteer militia that drilled at Garland and got called out when there was an emergency. They were prospectors, shopkeepers, hardscrabble farmers—they might have been good fighters, but they weren't the kind of men that took orders easily.

With that in mind, Fargo returned his lake-blue eyes to the shouting sergeant who appeared to be in command.

"What hostile uprising?"

"The Jicarilla are on the warpath. They cut off the Taos road and butchered everybody in Ojo Caliente. They burned out San Francisco last night."

The San Francisco he was talking about was a village, even smaller than San Luis, that sat about three miles up Culebra Creek. You could almost see it from the plaza here, and if anything up there was burning, you'd notice it just by looking east. All that was over there was Culebra Peak poking into the clear sky.

Fargo mentioned that to the sergeant.

"Damn you, obey my orders," he shouted back. "Now get inside so you can be safe while we protect your town and go teach the murderous Apaches a lesson."

"Just who are you to be telling me where to go?" Fargo asked, his temper rising.

"Sergeant Derek van Hoorn, in command of this detachment. That satisfy you?"

"And just where did you hear that the Jicarilla were rampaging?"

"What's it to you? Get your ass inside and out of our way, or we'll do it for you. Got that?"

Fargo shook his head. "If the Jicarilla were out plundering where you say they were, don't you think people here would have heard about it?" He turned to the local blacksmith. "Manuel, is the road to Taos cut off?"

The husky smith looked as though he'd rather do anything than get into the middle of this, but at Fargo's supportive nod, he answered. "No, *señor*. Two wagons came through this very morning, up from Fernández de Taos. They would not have been here if the road was closed. And other passing riders did not say that Ojo Caliente was—"

Sergeant van Hoorn cut him off. "What do you know, you ignorant peasant?"

"More than you do," Fargo shot back. "You say that San Francisco has been burned out, and you don't even trust the nose on your own face. If it was burning, we'd be smelling the smoke here. I don't smell anything except a bunch of lies, and I know just where they're coming from."

Van Hoorn seemed to think that was insulting, the way he whirled with the drawn saber. Fargo didn't have time to draw his Colt; the best he could do was suck in his stomach, so that the whizzing tip just sliced his shirt, before lunging forward with plans to get a bear hug around this manic sergeant. Once the man was pinned to the ground, maybe he'd start talking sense.

Right now, however, he wanted to fight. He spun sideways at Fargo's lunge, extending his free arm to jab the Trailsman's belly and keep him at a distance.

Fargo grabbed the offending arm and twisted, bringing up a boot that slammed against the back of van Hoorn's nearest knee. As he started to topple, the sergeant shouted orders that Fargo ought to be arrested if he wasn't shot first, but his men were too busy enjoying the fight to pay any heed to the command. Instead, they were cheering the Trailsman on; as with most volunteer outfits, discipline was worse than lax.

As van Hoorn went down, he tried another slash with the saber. Its sharp edge glanced against Fargo's arm, leaving a blood-edged slit in his sleeve. He gritted his teeth and sent a roundhouse left into van Hoorn's jaw. The sergeant's head snapped as his eyes blinked. That was enough of an opening for Fargo's knee to press itself against the sergeant's stomach with breath-robbing force.

Van Hoorn had lost, but he hadn't quite figured that out yet. He thrashed again with the saber, but this time, Fargo's left hand had a vise clamp on the soldier's forearm. With a savage twist that made things snap inside, the Trailsman forced van Hoorn to drop the sword.

Then the angry sergeant tried bringing up his other hand, two fingers extended, to poke out Fargo's eyes. Fargo saw it coming and rocked his head back, mouth agape. When the fingers arrived, his teeth clamped down. Just for good measure, the Trailsman bounced up and down a couple times, and on his last rise, he let go of the bleeding hand and came down with his knees, his full weight pounding into the sergeant's heaving chest.

Although van Hoorn had to be hurting with every breath, the man was still game. Both his arms clawed toward the Trailsman, and Fargo had to sidle off a bit, grab an arm, twist it hard, and roll the man so that he was belly-down. With Fargo on his back, pulling the man's head back at an angle that was just slightly less than what it would take to snap his neck, van Hoorn finally settled down a bit.

"Okay, Sergeant, do you see any Apaches? Where the hell did you hear that they were raiding?"

"A rider came to the fort last night." Van Hoorn was gasping between words, sometimes in the middle of them, so Fargo released the pressure, enough so that the man could talk more clearly. "His horse was all lathered. He said he came from the south, where the Apache were up in arms. So we called out our troops and at sunup we rode out."

Shit. These damn rumors were turning out to be mighty potent, maybe more than Fargo could handle with his own skills and weapons. There were rumors in San Luis that the survey party was going to take their land. Now this, which had pulled the soldiers away from Garland, leaving the surveyors without protection.

They shouldn't need any, considering that they had settled matters with the Utes, but a lot of things happened that shouldn't.

"Where are the surveyors?" Fargo demanded.

"Just north of the fort," van Hoorn gasped. "They started running their lines this morning, when we rode out."

Damn. "Who was that rider who told you there was an Indian uprising? Did anybody know him?"

Fargo couldn't see van Hoorn's nod, but he could feel it. The Trailsman lifted his hands and began to stand, carefully because van Hoorn might reach for one of his boots and trip him.

But the sergeant just lay there heaving for a few seconds, then rolled over and sat up, still collecting his breath and looking anguished every time he tried to inhale deeply.

"The rider? Of course I knew him. He was Pieter, my own brother."

"He's in the army too?"

Van Hoorn looked green around the gills until somebody brought him a canteen. Even then, he had to swallow about half of the water before he could continue. "No. He just came West a few months ago."

"What's he doing?"

Van Hoorn shook his head and massaged a bruised cheek. "He works for some big company that has offices in New York and Amsterdam. They were looking for western investments and sent him out to examine the prospects. That's what he told me, anyway, when he rode into Garland. It was a surprise to see him, but now, shit . . ."

Fargo helped the crestfallen sergeant to his feet. "You don't know what to believe, right?"

Van Hoorn nodded, but still seemed to have trouble keeping his feet under him. "My own brother tells me there are Apache raids. I believe him, of course. Then, it turns out that there aren't any Apache, I guess. No trouble at all, and I ride in here like there's a damn war going on, blind and foolish as can be. I don't know, I don't know."

Fargo led the sergeant toward the cantina. "This won't be much consolation, but a lot of us have been acting blind and foolish lately. Something's up, but I can't figure out what."

"You mean the efforts to stop the survey? Captain Macomber mentioned something."

"Damn right," Fargo agreed. "And—"

"And right now their guide is down here, twenty miles away, and so are any soldiers that might protect them." Van Hoorn shuddered. "Jesus, they're sitting ducks right now." He straightened with what had to be a considerable effort, then looked crestfallen. Most of his command, being neighbors who knew folks in San Luis, had pretty well melted away since the fight. Their mounts were hitched around the plaza, but few of the men were within sight.

"We've got to ride back up there. Pronto. And my men have vanished. It'll be dark before we can start moving again. If I can move at all." He clutched his belly and sagged against the adobe wall, near the door where the sounds of boisterous men were carried outside.

Now that some of the wine was wearing off, Fargo could feel a few places where he had been hit, and the thin slash on his arm was smarting. "Let's round up everyone we can and get as far as we can before those damn surveyors get themselves killed."

Van Hoorn nodded, although it was obvious that he wasn't in any condition to ride. Even if the man had made the understandable mistake of trusting his own brother, however, he was a dedicated soldier who would do his duty.

"Guess so, Fargo." His face turned gray as he leaned against the wall. "I'm going to get a drink or two first, though. Any Taos Lightning in there?"

Fargo nodded. After van Hoorn stumbled inside, Fargo found Gallegos and explained the situation. Within twenty minutes, the alcalde and his townsmen had rounded up all the volunteer soldiers from Garland and about a dozen other men who had decided to come along.

The bugler had already drank too much Taos Lightning to sound the call properly, but even though he sputtered terribly, the force assembled, and began to ride north in the lengthening shadows.

9

Although the sky was still bright, the sun had been swallowed by the haze-shrouded San Juan Mountains far to the west of Fort Garland. As the volunteer troopers dismounted and tended to their horses, Sergeant van Hoorn reluctantly went off to explain matters to the acting post commander, Wilburn Archer, a nervous young first lieutenant who must have had a close relative in the U.S. Congress, or perhaps some of General Winfield Scott's old love letters hidden in a bank vault somewhere. That was the only reasonable explanation as to why someone so stammering and indecisive was in charge of a frontier post.

But Fargo stayed in the orderly room only long enough to make sure that he and van Hoorn were telling the same story, and then sought out Captain Macomber, who had turned an adobe barracks building into his temporary headquarters.

The survey boss was sitting at a table, poring over some papers, when he rose to greet Fargo and to apply a match to a coal-oil lamp. "It looks like you ran into some trouble returning that woman to her family." Macomber smiled.

"Something like that." Fargo accepted the offer of a chair. "I'm not too sure what happened. But I was down there, then the soldiers showed up—which means that your crew was without much protection today. Where are they?"

Macomber's face fell. "We had two parties out in the field today. They should be getting back anytime now if they're not here already. You think they're in danger?"

Fargo nodded. "What were they doing?"

The captain motioned for Fargo to join him in looking at a rough pencil-sketch map of the San Luis Valley, which sat next to a bunch of other papers.

"One crew should be close by. They started early this morning right at the surveyor's monument that's next to the post flagpole. We know where it is, in relationship to the general land-office surveys that tie to the principal meridian through New Mexico. They were going to run lines north for a couple miles, till they got to the township line, and then west for as far as they could, marking section corners as they went along."

"How far do you think they got?"

"On flat land, without any trees or rivers to get in the way, a good crew can handle better than a dozen miles a day. They're supposed to stay at it until we establish a corner for the Espinoza grant. Then we can tie that corner to the regular national grid, and we'll be able to put the Espinoza grant on the map."

Fargo glanced at the map and pointed to an area north and west of the fort with many small lakes and a lot of scribbling. "The corner of the grant would be up there somewhere?"

"Somewhere." Macomber laughed. "I've been trying to translate the property description. Most of it's pretty easy to follow, except for where we start: La Laguna de los Patos."

"Duck Lake." Fargo searched his memory. "Lot of little lakes up north of those sand dunes, and I suppose that ducks stop at most of them when it's time to head north for the summer or south for the winter."

Macomber started to say something, but it was muffled by the sudden arrival sounds outside on the parade ground. The captain beat Fargo to the door, where both looked out to see that one survey party had returned.

"They were the ones running the line today," Macomber explained. "In a day or two, they'll be so far along that we'll have to leave the fort and set up camp, but I decided that if the fort is here, we might as well use it. Miserable as these barracks are, they're certainly better than tents."

Fargo was tempted to relax, but then remembered that there was still another party out there. "Where did the others go, the ones that aren't back yet? How many were there?"

Macomber returned to the table, Fargo at his side. "It might be easier to show you than to tell you." He pointed to the map, as well as his scrawled translation of the Mexican grant document.

"The Espinoza grant starts at Duck Lake, according to this. The idea in these new surveys is to figure out what the first person to lay out the land did, and follow in his footsteps with modern equipment to tie that old survey into the national grid. The problem with a lake, however, is where do you start? One bank or the other? In the middle? And of all those damn little lakes up there, which one is Duck Lake? That's why I sent the second crew up north today—to ask around and to look around. Somebody that lives around here might know which lake they call Duck Lake. Or maybe there's a lake up there that just obviously has to be Duck Lake—could be that there's one pond where some ducks stay all year, and that's why it got the name."

Fargo didn't like the sinking feeling that crawled into his belly and wouldn't leave. "So you sent a few of your crew north, hoping they'd discover Duck Lake. And once you knew where that was, you could start the formal survey of the grant boundaries."

"Anything wrong with that?"

The Trailsman stood and shook his head ominously.

"Just that somebody is trying to stop your survey, and you sent men into the field unprotected. I wasn't around, and neither were any soldiers. They're not back yet, and it's dark now, which means there's not much chance of even looking for them before morning."

Macomber stood, his face growing pale. "I didn't think they'd be in any particular danger."

"Maybe they're not," Fargo conceded. "But I'd certainly feel a lot better if they were back."

"So would I. Isn't there anything we can do?"

Fargo stepped toward the door and savored the cool night air that seeped through its cracks. "That's the problem with looking for people at night. The only way you'll find them, unless you're just lucky, is if they've built a fire. And if they were able to build a fire, chances are they don't need finding—they're doing just fine on their own."

Their ruminations were interrupted by more noises out in the parade ground. Fargo hoped it was returning surveyors, but the ruckus was just one of the crew members running out of an adjacent barracks, accompanied by a lot of derisive hooting and hollering from behind.

"What the hell is going on out here?" Macomber bellowed while Fargo chased after the running crew member.

"We don't want anybody giving us lice," a shout boomed from the barracks. "Swanson's filthy, and he won't take a bath. So we were going to make him take one."

Macomber headed toward the barracks to sort things out. Near the flagpole, Fargo caught up to Swanson, who wasn't running all that fast on account of a game leg. He recognized Swanson as the one who'd been wounded in the shin during the Ute attack over on the other side of the pass.

Gene Swanson didn't seem all that filthy or louse-ridden when the Trailsman's big arm hooked around his neck and brought the panting chainman to a halt.

"What's going on?" Gene gasped, trying to get his bare feet under him.

"You tell me," Fargo grunted. "All I know is what I heard, which is that they're taking baths in there, and you're not." He glanced back at the barracks, where the door still stood open. Past Macomber, who stood in the frame and gave soft-spoken orders, there was a hot cast-iron stove, its top covered with kettles and pots of heating water. Beside it sat a hairy-shouldered young man in a galvanized washtub, and Fargo could spot a few others standing around, in robes and various stages of undress.

"I take baths," Swanson insisted in a husky whisper. "I keep myself clean."

His nostrils had confirmed that, so Fargo released the hold from Swanson's lean neck. "That may be," Fargo said, "but . . ." He didn't get a chance to finish, because Swanson had taken off running again.

With a flying tackle that caught Swanson's knees, Fargo brought him down. They tumbled into cactus and the scattered rocks that dotted this land. Swanson's bare foot kicked harmlessly at the Trailsman's abdomen, and the chainman writhed in an effort to shake his grip. He managed to twist around so that he was on his back before Fargo got his grip moved up to the young man's shoulders.

Swanson tried to buck him off. Fargo tightened his grasp into a bear hug and almost fell off in astonishment. He felt a pair of breasts pressed against him. They were bound by wrapped cloth or something under the baggy cotton shirt, but the sensation was unmistakable. It quickly dawned on Fargo just why Swanson hadn't wanted to take a bath with the other men.

The Trailsman leaned his head forward and whispered into Swanson's ear. "My apologies, ma'am. Let me help you to your feet."

He rolled off and, with a vice clamp on a shoulder,

pulled Swanson up with him. The chainman's curly hair sagged into his chest. "How did you know?" she sobbed.

Fargo laughed. "I should have guessed sooner. When you were wounded in the leg, you were real picky about your treatment, especially about taking off any clothes. Your voice isn't all that deep. I saw you go through the motions of shaving one morning, but it didn't look like you were at all serious about it. You'd rather get shamed and humiliated than take off your clothes in a room full of men, and once I was on top of you down there and holding you . . . well, that removed all doubts. Now, who are you really?"

Her head pressed harder at his chest. "Jean Swanson is my real name."

Fargo didn't know whether to believe that or not. Too many weird things were happening. Already one of their party, Red, had turned out to be a turncoat. Then another woman had sabotaged their efforts, and Fargo had been kept from the survey party when he might be needed. But he decided that even if Jean Swanson traveled under false colors, she wasn't part of that. When you sent in people to play undercover games, you made them as much like the others as possible. Nobody would send in a woman masquerading as a man, but it was best to be sure.

"Let's go for a walk," he suggested.

Her hand dropped down and clutched his. "You won't tell anybody, will you?"

"I don't plan to, but I do want to hear what you have to say about this."

They strolled along a wagon road that circled the fort, about a quarter-mile from the buildings. "I want to be a surveyor," she explained. "And the only way to learn the profession is to apprentice. No surveyor back home would take a woman as an apprentice, as a rodman, chainman, or ax man." She fell silent as a sentry approached.

Fargo assured the man that they were not Ute raiders, and turned his attention back to Jean. "Why would anybody want to be a surveyor?" he wondered. He couldn't think of anything that sounded more boring.

"Because I'm quick with numbers," she whispered. "That's one place to put that to use."

"Isn't there anyplace else you could use that talent? Teaching school, maybe?"

She bristled. "Who's ever heard of any stupid old schoolmarm? None of them ever amounted to anything. Surveyors are important, powerful people."

They had never struck Fargo as anything except dull little men that squinted through theodolites and then stayed up half the night, making field notes by candlelight. "Really?" he questioned.

"Certainly," she huffed, her voice rising an octave now that she didn't have to pretend to be male. "George Washington was a surveyor. So was Thomas Jefferson. President Lincoln used to survey when he lived in the back country of Illinois."

"Seems to me that most of those prominent men were lawyers," Fargo reminded.

"I'll never live long enough to see the day when a woman can be an attorney," she moaned. "I can become a regular surveyor, though, and then I can do things. I'll make maps. I'll be remembered."

"Who remembers mapmakers and surveyors?"

They were about halfway around the fort now, and Fargo still had no idea what to do once they got back to the main entry. Maybe Macomber would have got the others settled down, and after that, her problem here would be like the rest of life—a day-to-day struggle. But keeping her gender a secret wouldn't be his struggle, anyway.

"They're the only ones who really get remembered," Jean insisted. "Columbus did the sailing and exploring, but we call this continent America, don't we? In honor of Amerigo Vespucci, who never explored anything. But he was the mapmaker, and it's his name that got put on the New World. It's surveyors who determine how high mountains are, and they put their names on them. Just before I left Minnesota, I read that the British are considering naming the highest mountain in the world, between India and China, in honor of Sir George Everest. He was surveyor-general of India from 1823 to 1843."

She probably had more to say, but Fargo interrupted. "Okay, I see your point. You want to be a surveyor. Just why isn't all that important."

"What's that supposed to mean?"

"Nothing. It's just that people want what people want. That's what matters. They always come up with the reasons later. They pretend that they've thought things through before deciding what they want, but almost always, I'd bet it's the other way around. The decision comes before the reason."

She straightened for a moment, then sighed and leaned her head against his shoulder, and her grip on his hand got more friendly. "I suppose that is true. But what am I to do? This was my great opportunity to learn the surveyor's science, but how am I going to deal with those men in the barracks? They're hardly men, really. They're fresh out of college, most of them, and high-spirited. If they ever discovered the truth about me, I'll never be safe from them and I'll probably get sent home."

"No you won't."

"How can you be so sure?"

"Because first off, you're about two hundred miles from where they might find anybody else to do your job, so they're pretty well stuck with you. Second, your secret is safe with me, though I don't know how much longer you're going to be able to fool them. Third, I'm on your side here. If they give you any trouble, I'll shove it back down their throats. Fourth, if you do get dismissed, then I'll just hire you as my assistant. As the guide, I can do that. So quit worrying."

"That's quite a list." Jean giggled. "Okay, I'll quit worrying. I'll just go back to the barracks and hope that Captain Macomber has settled everybody down. I'll have to come up with some story, though, as to why I wouldn't bathe there."

Fargo thought about that. "Tell them it has something to do with that wound, that you're not supposed to get it wet."

They were back at the main gate now, and Fargo asked the sentry whether the other party had returned. He hadn't heard any hoofbeats during the walk, but his mind had been focused on other matters.

"No, Mr. Fargo. Nobody's come or gone, except you and him."

"Shit," the Trailsman grumbled. He hated the idea of venturing into this overwhelming darkness, but it would be even worse to stay at the fort, sitting around worrying all night. Fargo usually wasn't like that, but this survey seemed to be jinxed, and until he found out where the trouble was coming from, and put a stop to it, he was bound to feel edgy.

With Jean at his side, Fargo returned to Macomber's quarters, where a lantern still glowed.

"What is it, Fargo?" He paused. "I see you found the runaway chainman."

The Trailsman nodded. "I'm going to head north to see if I can find our Duck Lake party. How many were there?"

"Three. Waters, Swearingen, and Cohen. Jesus, I hope they're all right."

"So do I." Fargo paused and hoped his mouth wouldn't stay so dry. "Is it all right if I take Swanson here with me? I might need some help."

Macomber nodded. "Sure. You have any advice for tomorrow? I'd sure like to get more of that line run if we can. The weather's good right now, and . . ."

"If you can get a few soldiers to go with you," Fargo responded. "In fact, you might see if you can get a troop to patrol north in the morning following our tracks. It might simplify matters, depending on what we run into."

"I'm not in the chain of command here," Macomber pointed out. "But I outrank Lieutenant Archer, and I'll pull rank if I have to. Anything else?"

"Wish us luck."

Over at the stables, Fargo woke the night hostler. The Ovaro had already been ridden twenty miles today, and nobody knew what tomorrow might bring. Fargo signed for three government mules. One was for Swanson, one got a packsaddle with some gear, and the other was a spare, just in case.

The Big Dipper hung directly above the polestar. This time of year, that meant it was about midnight, with better than five hours until any light appeared in the east.

The Ovaro settled into an easy walk as Fargo and Jean Swanson rode abreast, navigating by the stars and by the gurgling sounds that Trinchera Creek made as it tumbled westward toward the Rio Grande.

They left the creek to swing north around some bluffs, and when they were close enough to hear the waters of the Rio Grande, Fargo headed north. Duck Lake was up there somewhere. Most of those lakes sat at the edge of a vast field of dunes, which looked like a beach without an ocean. The hills of fine-grained sand had been piled up against the Sangre de Cristos by the savage winds that often raked across this dry valley floor. Given how porous that made this valley floor, many lakes came and went, depending on how wet each spring was.

Something that would be named Duck Lake probably held water every fall, though. The biggest permanent ponds had other names, Head Lake and San Luis Lake. Fargo recalled another one a mile or two from the familiar route that ran north to Poncha Pass from Taos, San Luis, and Fort Garland. Did the lake have a name? And if so, was it Duck Lake? He couldn't remember. A few years ago, when he'd last seen it, there were ducks swimming on its surface and waddling around its reedy shore, but in the fall, that didn't mean a lot.

"Fargo, we're going to Duck Lake, aren't we?" Jean had so far ridden in silence, much to Fargo's pleasure. There were times to talk, but this wasn't one of them. He needed to do some thinking.

"That's where we'll start, anyway," he muttered, annoyed at the interruption.

"Just before they left, Jed Waters said he had talked to some of the garrison at the fort. He got the idea that the Duck Lake they were looking for was almost due west of Mosca Pass, on the west side of the wagon road to Saguache."

That would be the same lake. "Sounds about right," he grunted. "About all we can do is get close to it, though, until it gets light enough to see our way around."

Jean whispered her agreement and caught his desire not to talk. Fargo just slumped in his saddle, getting as much rest as he could.

A new day finally got under way with a pinkish glow in the east, where the jagged summits of the Sangres formed irregular saw teeth that pressed against the sky.

As soon as they could make out a few landmarks, he reined up. They were atop a low rise. To his right, the meandering San Luis Creek came to an end, its waters flowing slowly into Head Lake, where they would sink into the sand and emerge in other nearby lakes that appeared wherever there were low spots.

He hoped Duck Lake would be three or four miles to the left. Wordlessly, he urged the Ovaro that way. It wasn't until they crested the rise at the rim of the bowl around the lake that Jean said anything.

Then she screamed and cried for several minutes before regaining her composure. Fargo didn't blame her.

While a flock of summer-resident ducks paddled placidly in the dawn, bobbing up and down for their breakfast, Fargo dismounted. Taking care to avoid disturbing any tracks, he walked gingerly to a spit of sand that stuck out into the lake.

Fargo recognized Jed Waters by the fastidious man's kid-leather boots, which he always kept polished. He was lying facedown, and the back of his head had been blown off. Some of the gore had spattered against Vance Swearingen, a short, husky blond chainman. He gaped at the sky with sightless eyes and a hole in his chest. The other member of the party, dark-haired Simon Cohen, was some distance away, up on the bank. His death bullet had caught him in the back, right between the shoulder blades.

From appearances, the men were lying where they had fallen. Fargo looked for a spot that would have been good to shoot from, and spotted some brush forty yards away, on the far side of the lake.

Each body showed evidence of just one shot. Fargo tried to envision the scene. The trio must have been out on the spit. There must have been two bushwhackers; one bullet got Waters and one got Swearingen, at almost the same instant. These were heavy rounds, so they had likely come from the same kind of gun Fargo carried, a single-shot Sharps carbine. When the shooting started, Cohen had headed for cover, hoping to fight back. He had the only weapon among the three, a light Colt navy pistol that was still clutched in his hand. One of the bushwhackers had nailed him, just a step or two away from some brush that might have saved him.

Cohen had also carried the notebook, which indicated that they believed that they had found the Duck Lake that formed a corner of the Espinoza grant.

The men had been riding mules, which were nowhere in sight. They had also carried a few light instruments of their craft, but those weren't anywhere to be found, either.

There were tracks in the sandy soil, however, and Fargo decided to find out where they went after sending Jean back to the fort with the news.

10

"I'm scared to ride back to Garland by myself," Jean confessed. Another shudder, either from fear or from revulsion at the sight of the three bodies, swept across her lean form as she stood above Duck Lake, holding the reins of her mule. "I never thought I'd encounter anything like this . . ." Her voice trailed off.

Fargo handed her the Ovaro's reins and stepped around the pond to the brush where the shots had come from. Working uphill in the sandy soil, he found the tracks of two men. The shorter one—about five foot six, judging by the length of his stride—wore low-heeled boots. The taller, almost the Trailsman's height but with less bulk, had been wearing moccasins or something similar.

Given the man's height and how short the local Utes, Apaches, and Comanches were, it wasn't likely that an Indian had been involved, though. A lot of men on the frontier preferred moccasins because they fit more comfortably than all but the best custom-made boots.

That was about all Fargo could learn from those impressions in the dirt, so he began to circle the small lake, looking for any other tracks that would show clearly in the low-angled light of the just-risen sun. The bushwhackers' horses had been tied down in the next draw. The narrow U-shaped prints came from the surveyors' mules, which had been down by the lake.

From the look of things, the mules had been taken by the ambushers after the shooting.

All the tracks went east, almost directly into the sun. For an hour or two, even the smallest disturbance on the ground would produce a shadow. That would make tracking easy, but then again, with the sun in your eyes, you had trouble seeing ahead, and Fargo would be riding toward some people who had just killed three men in cold blood.

However, the trail wasn't going to get any warmer while Fargo waited for the sun to rise to a more favorable position. While the ducks greeted the day's warmth with a hoarse chorus of quacks, he motioned for Jean to bring the mules and the Ovaro and join him.

"I can't say I blame you for not wanting to ride back on your own," he conceded as he checked his weapons. "Can you shoot?"

"I grew up on a farm and had five brothers. I've hunted some," she explained. "But only with a small rifle, never anything as powerful as a Sharps."

"But you could shoot one if you had to," Fargo prodded.

She nodded. "Live and learn."

"Then we're going to track down the ambushers that just killed three of our crew," Fargo announced as he swung aboard the Ovaro.

Jean shuddered again, but ended up with a resolute expression. Her hazel eyes bored at Fargo. "Aren't you going to bury those men? Or do something with the bodies?" She concluded with sarcasm, "Scalp them, perhaps, as you did with the others?"

Fargo waited until they were on an easy eastward trot before answering. "I don't need scalps now. And if we leave the bodies out, then the buzzards will start circling any minute now." He turned, as she did, and saw that the first vultures had already arrived at Duck Lake. "They're supposed to be sending some soldiers up this way from Garland today. The troopers will see the vultures in the sky, head for the lake, and if they're any good at reading sign, they'll figure out what happened. They'll do the same thing we're doing."

Jean nodded, then smiled in comprehension. "So we'll have those soldiers to back us up if we run into trouble." She shook her head. "I'm beginning to see why the scout gets paid so much, more than any of the surveyors. You're always thinking ahead, aren't you?"

"I try," Fargo replied. "But nobody can think of everything. Life is full of surprises, and you just have to do your best to keep from getting surprised to death when something new pops up."

The tracks veered northward for several easy miles, joined the valley's main wagon road, and then swung east. The trail of horse and mule prints dropped across a gentle draw for the ford of the meandering San Luis Creek. Fargo paused to stare hard at the tracks on the far side. Satisfied that no one had remained in ambush at the crossing, he proceeded. Just across the far swell, the wagon road forked.

The more-used branch continued north. The other trended to the east, and it had the tracks Fargo wanted to follow. That was a relief. If the bushwhackers had gone to Saguache, their tracks would be lost in the other traffic and they could gain some time as Fargo tried to determine whether they had headed west over Cochetopa Pass, north across Poncha Pass, or east across Hayden Pass, the only practical northern crossing of the Sangres.

Near the top of the next rise, Fargo halted and told Jean to stay back, below the skyline. He edged forward in a crouch, Sharps ready.

About two miles off sat the headquarters of the Espinoza grant. A rambling log house, part of it with a second story, dominated the yard. Behind the house were a barn and several corrals, along with scattered outbuildings. A ditch coming down from the east provided water power for a small sawmill and its neighbor, a gristmill, where two men were loading sacked flour into a wagon. An open-fronted smithy faced Fargo, and in its shadows he could see the glowing coals amid the distant ringing of the blacksmith's steady hammering. One long ramshackle log structure, most likely a bunkhouse for the hired help, sat close by the house. Fargo saw all sorts of small movements, but then decided that the distant flutterings were just chickens scratching around the yard.

He scanned the corrals closely, and as he suspected, there wasn't any sign of the mules, even though their tracks plainly led that way. He crept back and held the horses so that Jean could sneak forward for a view. Then, staying below the ridge, they continued east.

"If the tracks go straight down to that settlement," she wondered, "why don't we just go down there?"

"For one thing, we'd be outnumbered," Fargo muttered, hating to explain the obvious. "For another, the mules aren't down there. Which means that whoever's running things there is involved."

That obviously didn't seem logical to Jean, who looked perplexed for about a mile of country that was getting wetter and rougher as they approached the abrupt west flank of the jagged Sangres.

Jean examined the mountain wall and turned to the Trailsman. "They're an odd part of the Rocky Mountain chain," she commented.

Fargo scanned the precipitous blue-gray barricade of jagged peaks that stretched endlessly southward. "They're about the longest range I can think of," he noted. "From the Arkansas River to south of Santa Fe—the range must be two hundred miles long, and the Sangres have to be the narrowest range in the West. No foothills or anything. They just rear up between two reasonably flat valleys, and I bet it's not twenty miles from one side to the other."

Jean nodded. "That's typical of fault-block mountains like these and the Tetons."

"What-block mountains?"

"Fault-block. It's like a part of the earth's crust

tipped on its side, like this." She made explanatory motions with her hands—they were long-fingered, the way women's hands were supposed to be, but she had picked up plenty of calluses and scrapes during her masquerade as a man.

After Fargo's nod of comprehension, she went on, glad to demonstrate that there was something she knew more about than Fargo did. "From what I have read, the Sangre de Cristos may be the youngest mountains around here."

"Why's that?"

"Many of the summits have outcrops of sedimentary rock, such as limestone, which is relatively soft."

Fargo mulled on that. "So if they'd been sticking up there for any length of time, the soft rock would have been worn away by wind and water, leaving the harder stuff on top. Sounds reasonable."

Jean had a new announcement. "There is evidence that these mountains are still rising."

"As we ride here?"

"Not exactly. Something deep in the earth is still pushing them up, but other forces hold them in place. Every so often, the deep force builds up to where something snaps. There's an earthquake, and the mountains rise a few feet higher."

"Come to think of it," Fargo recalled, "I've heard the local Utes tell tales they heard from their grandfathers about days that the earth shook and how they couldn't figure out what sins they had committed that got their gods that mad at them."

As they stopped at a creek to let their mounts relax and drink some water, Jean grew silent, and the perplexed look returned for several minutes before her knowing smile returned.

"I think I see why you didn't go to the ranch. Suppose I ran that ranch. Two men show up at night, with some government mules. They either say they're with Uncle Sam, or else that they found the mules wandering loose and wanted somebody to take them in until the army or whoever asked for them. I'd go along with that, not knowing any better. If I knew about those cold-blooded assassinations, though, then I'd want those mules, and the men who came with them, to be long gone before any nosy outsiders showed up."

"Exactly." Fargo smiled. "Now, if my guess is right, we'll pick up those mule tracks again, along one of these creeks that comes down out of the mountains."

If Fargo had been trying to hide some murderers and stolen mules, he'd have gone farther north, perhaps up Deadman or Crestone creeks. Up at their headwaters were trail passes, gaps that simplified getting over to the Wet Mountain Valley, where you had a lot of choices about where to hide next—Canon City, the Pueblo, even north to South Park if you knew where to ford the Arkansas. But these men had been in a hurry, and he found their sign climbing alongside the main fork of Sand Creek as it tumbled out of a narrow rock-lined cleft.

The Trailsman dismounted and examined the tracks carefully. Earlier, they had shown signs of haste—the impressions were deep and hard-struck, and small rocks had been tossed up. Now the pace had slowed. Part of it had to be that they were in rougher country, but that didn't explain it all. Fargo developed a timetable.

The surveyors had been shot early yesterday afternoon, Fargo decided. The ambushers had gone to the ranch, an easy two-hour ride. They'd spend an hour or so at the ranch before continuing into the mountains. Darkness would set in shortly thereafter.

At first light today, they'd have pressed on, since from this area, the smoke of a campfire would be visible from the roads in the valley. So this wasn't the place to hide. Instead, they would press on until they found a secluded high basin to hole up in.

In this country of narrow canyons and jutting ridges, ambush was always a possibility, but the bushwhackers would presume that they had at least a day's start on any pursuers. From up here, where there were frequent sweeping views of the valley floor, they might even be able to spot the vultures—and as long as the buzzards were going at Duck Lake, they would know that their crime had not been discovered. So they wouldn't be too concerned about being trailed. In all probability, they weren't expecting company this soon, and they wouldn't be real diligent about looking for it.

Even so, Fargo cautioned Jean to remain wary, to scan the ridges frequently for any glint of sunshine on metal, to pay heed if her mule seemed edgy, and to stay loose in her saddle so she could roll off in an instant.

"Going with you is hardly what I'd call a pleasure ride," she commented dryly. "You know more things to worry about than any other man I've known. Don't you ever relax?"

"Once in a while," Fargo grunted. "On a featherbed, in a woman's arms. But that's about the size of it. And even then . . ." He recalled how quickly pleasure had changed into trouble, back at the Bent's Old Fort, when Señora Espinoza's husband had arrived, pistol in hand.

Jean blushed at his statement. "Then you won't have any opportunity to relax on this trip."

"You're right," Fargo agreed. "I don't know of any featherbeds close by." He ignored her spluttering and bellicose glare as he swung out of the saddle and knelt next to a rock-rimmed fire pit.

The men they were following obviously hadn't been trying to cover their tracks, which would have been impossible anyway, with two horses and three mules in this seldom-traveled country.

The fire had been doused with a hatful of creekwater, and the ashes were still quite damp. So there had been a fire early this morning. Fargo glanced at his short shadow; it was close to noon. They were within six hours of the bushwhackers.

Fargo stifled a yawn as well as an intense desire to rekindle this fire and brew the pot of coffee he craved after being up all night.

Among the ashes was a piece of charred cloth, likely a cotton bandanna that had fallen into the flames. He could still make out some of the pattern. That might be useful for asking questions later, so he stuffed it into his pocket.

They continued eastward, climbing a steep trail that twisted through the looming trees, sometimes right next to the creek and, where it ran through small chasms, as far as a quarter-mile away. When they were behind the first row of peaks, the valley swung so that it paralleled the range. Now, close to timberline, it seemed suspended between two jagged gray ridges.

It looked like a good spot for holing up, but Fargo's cautious eyes disclosed no sign of life other than the usual frolicking marmots. Over at the far edge of this basin, an unmistakable trail zigzagged across a steep field of scree, crossing the ridge between two ragged summits, so high that they still held some of last winter's snow in scattered ravines.

If there was a valley like this over on the other side, then that's where the bushwhackers and the mules would be, Fargo decided. They rode to where the trail steepened. To Jean's dismay, he announced it was time to walk and lead their mounts.

After what seemed like a century of slow, quiet walking, with sharp rocks poking at their soles, they reached the pass. Indeed, there was a secluded basin below them, rimmed by peaks. The mule tracks led on down the trail. Fargo's lake-blue eyes traced the path, down into the trees, where he looked futilely for any sign of the ambushers. He guessed something was amiss, though, or the jaybirds would be fluttering about and chirping at one another.

When he looked up, however, he realized why the birds were so quiet. Boiling black clouds had hidden the sun, and a cold wind clawed at his beard. Shit. In about thirty minutes, or maybe less, the customary mountain afternoon thunderstorm would commence. Not only would there be cold rain that could crawl right into your bones and freeze you, there would also be bruising hail and tremendous bolts of lightning.

Getting into the trees would help, perhaps, though they wouldn't be all that safe from lightning. The best cover would be amid the rocks.

As if she could read his mind, Jean said something to the effect that most of this was limestone, which sometimes held caves, and she sure wanted to be in one right now.

Fargo scanned the basin again, especially the edges above timberline. He looked for hollow spots, places where water trickled down from the rocks, anything that might indicate a hole where they might take shelter. Although he knew he had never been here before, something looked familiar about the place. He couldn't figure out just what, though, and there was more pressing business on his mind.

Jean pointed toward a depressed jumble of rocks, several hundred yards away, down a little and to the right. That looked as good as anything else they were likely to find in time. So, Fargo nodded and they scampered that way, stepping cautiously through the talus.

A few drops had plunked against Fargo's hat by the time they got there. This was a relief. Two little ribs of solid rock, about five yards apart, jutted out of the mountain. Between them was a pile of fallen rock. Where they began to close together was an inky hole, perhaps four feet high and half as wide. If it went back any distance at all, at least he and Jean would be sheltered.

While Jean held the horses, Fargo crept forward. Stale-smelling air emerged from the opening, so it went back a ways. He waved her toward him, then started in as the storm began to get serious about refilling all the local creeks and lakes.

Fargo's probing revealed that the opening was smaller than the cave's passage. Once he was a yard or so inside, he could stand up straight. This chamber, though, extended back only six or seven feet. Then the floor seemed to vanish. Between thunderclaps, Fargo tossed rocks and listened for their thunks. From what he could tell, the passage sloped steeply downward. It wasn't quite vertical, but it was close.

"Why are you so curious about this cave?" Jean wondered.

"Not much else to do, until things settle down out there," he grunted. "What did you do with our stock?"

"Pulled them in as close as I could," she responded as Fargo turned to see for himself.

Mostly he saw the Ovaro, standing in the pelting hail and glaring at a dry Fargo, but there was a good view of the basin, illuminated by frequent flashes of lightning. Some bolts soared from cloud to cloud, sending great peals of thunder across the valley in their wake. Others seemed to rise from the ground to meet flashes from the sky. Fargo felt his hair stand on end and reflexively held his breath as that happened, only twenty yards away. The farthest mule got real frisky about that, but Fargo decided that was the mule's problem.

As he looked past the mule, it finally dawned on Fargo why this valley seemed familiar. But he had to be sure. Now so eager that he hardly noticed the wind, rain, lightning, and hail, he sprang out to the pinto and grabbed the old parchment map from his saddlebags. Once it was in hand, he slipped on the wet jumbled rocks and stuck out a hand to steady himself against the jutting rib.

Another thunderclap from only a few yards away almost made him jump, but the flash of light revealed a pattern on the rock before Fargo's hand. The paint had long faded, but the thunderbolt image that etched itself into his mind was unmistakable—a Maltese cross.

Fargo kept that to himself after scrambling back to

the cave mouth and squatting next to Jean, where there was enough light for him to make out the markings on the parchment. Jean peered at it as he shifted it, finally aligning it with the basin out there—this had to be the valley.

But the cross on the map wasn't in quite the right place. They had barely crossed the ridge, and that cross sat quite a ways farther downslope. Of course, a map drawn from memory might not be all that accurate, and everything else fit. If that story were true, then somewhere in the cave that yawned at his back, there were about four hundred pounds of gold.

The storm was settling down to just a pounding rain as Jean rubbed her curly ear-length hair against his shoulder. "Skye, tell me about the map, please."

While the storm waned and the sun reemerged, he gave her the basics of the story as she cuddled against him.

"So there might be a fortune here?"

He shrugged. "It could be. If the story's true. And if somebody didn't get to it a long time ago."

This prolonged stooping had encouraged Fargo's back to start aching, and though that gold was tempting, it wasn't Fargo's job today. The idea was to catch those bushwhackers and make sure that they wouldn't bother the survey party again. While Jean went out to check on the mules, he sidled back for one last look at the chamber, just so he'd have a better idea of what he'd face whenever he came back.

Jean's shrill scream became muffled before it halted.

Fargo spun around and, drawing his Colt, sprang toward the opening, dropping into a crawl as he emerged.

Shit. His flitting glance took in the situation. The bushwhackers had been down in the valley, amid the trees. They must have spotted the exposed mules. While the storm waned and he and Jean had been talking about the map, the ambushers had worked their way up the mountainside. Now the shorter one had his arm hooked around Jean's throat. Any desire she had to wiggle or yell was dampened by the muzzle of the Remington pressed against her ear. Fargo recognized the man as one of those he had seen at Bent's Old Fort, part of the crew that had been with María Teresa Espinoza's aggrieved husband.

The other one, tall and blond, stood about ten feet away, atop the rib just above the cross. He had to be Sergeant van Hoorn's brother. Their faces were almost identical, except that Sergeant van Hoorn had never looked so cold, nor had he ever pointed a Sharps at the Trailsman.

"Just come on out, stand up straight, and unbuckle that gun belt real slow, Fargo, and let it drop," Pieter van Hoorn ordered. "Or this lady surveyor will get to join those three friends of hers that we got yesterday."

Fargo moved forward, then stood and blinked, as if from exhaustion and confusion, shaking his head slowly as if he didn't understand.

To make sure he did, the other man slowly thumbcocked the hammer on his revolver. The click sounded as loud as any thunder had. Fargo undid his belt.

Jean's captor grinned. He was missing several teeth and the remaining chompers were a muddy yellow. "Looks like we'll get some pleasure out of this one first. How was she, Fargo?"

Trying to stall for time, Fargo answered, "I wouldn't know. I've been a gentleman."

"Shit," van Hoorn spat. "Fargo, I know you by reputation. You have never been around a woman for more than twenty minutes without getting into her drawers. We saw that back at Bent's Old Fort."

The Ovaro stood placidly, almost within reach. Was there any way for him to get fractious, to start kicking and rearing, to create a distraction? No, that wouldn't help. As long as that pistol was jammed against Jean's ear, she would be dead the instant her captor felt at all flustered.

Jean's face was white with the terror of what might

happen to her. Maybe if she twisted and ducked, she could snap loose, and the reflexive shot would miss. Fargo could swoop up his Colt and they'd have at least a fighting chance. But a chance of what? Ducking back into the cave would be foolish, and out in these rocks they'd be exposed to lethal fire from two men who were dead shots. The two men would have to be taken out instantly and Fargo didn't see any way to do that.

His thoughts raced. He heard the rustle of a moccasin on rocks. Something sliced through the thin air. He looked up just in time for his nose and eyes to catch the stock of a heavy Sharps, swung with smashing, brutal force.

11

A rock poked at the groggy Trailsman's back, and the more he twisted, the deeper it stabbed at his spine. The grudging muscles of his shoulder burned as he tentatively eased his right hand back, in the instinctive hope that he could somehow sit up and escape that clawing rock. His hand pressed against a cold, wet surface and slid away. Gritting his teeth, Fargo pulled the hand back and felt for a handhold. A small depression kept the hand in place. He rolled and pressed, extending his arm.

He could feel himself sitting up. Now, to shake his head, open his eyes, awaken, and face this day. No, the world was sliding away as if he were a snowball in an avalanche. Once free of the rock, he began to bounce as he plummeted, arms thrashing for a grip, something to grab to halt, or even slow, this accelerating plunge down a steep slide of slick, wet rock.

No, he shouted, the sound swallowed by the blackness. Just let me wake up from this awful dream. But he knew he would wake in time. Dreams, no matter how nightmarish, always worked that way. You'd dream you were falling, but you always came awake before you hit anything. This fall wasn't like the others, because he wasn't plummeting through the air, he was sliding down a slick-rock ravine where there were bumps that jolted every bone in his body, but there was nothing to grab. Even the walls were as slick as greased glass when his flailing hands pawed at them. He gasped and gasped for air and there was hardly any, not enough to fill a man's lungs, just enough for a stale smell to keep getting stronger and stronger.

Fargo discovered that this wasn't a dream when his boots slammed into something hard, the jolt started in his ankles and reverberated clear up to the tip of his head, pausing along the way to make sure that his knees twisted, his spine was hammered, his ribs burned, and his neck vibrated in a dozen painful directions.

But he could sit up. He gulped in air, such as it was. Every breath made that dull pounding headache even worse. He blinked his eyes, and nothing happened. His eyelids seemed frozen, sewn shut. What was wrong?

The last thing he had seen was that rifle stock, fine-grained walnut inches away, and then covering everything, the wood turning into this inky blackness that had now settled over Fargo's entire world.

Blood. That was it. Naturally a man who got hit that way would gush blood all around his eye sockets. And if he'd been knocked out for any length of time, the blood would congeal, gluing his eyelashes down so that he couldn't force his eyelids to open. That made sense.

He felt for a bandanna, twisting to find it in his hip pocket. Slowly, he mopped both eyes out. He knew he'd succeeded because his eyelids seemed to scrape his eyeballs when he tried to blink.

Or at least he thought he was trying to blink. It didn't make a bit of difference whether his eyes were open or shut. Just a charcoal void, either way.

Shit. Those bastards had blinded him with that blow. Maybe not that blow precisely, since there may have been other brutal kicks and swings at someone who was knocked out, down and unable to fight back.

Blindness. Never to see another mountain sunset, prairie flower, or woman's smile. Never to find tracks or hunt game or . . . What the hell was he going to do? That was Fargo's life's work, the only thing he knew how to do—he could see things that most other people didn't even notice. But when your guide can't see? That would never do.

Stand around some little town with a tin cup, telling a hard-luck story, living on public sympathy? No, that wasn't fair, Fargo told himself. He'd met blind people who lived tolerable lives, making themselves useful. He tried to imagine life as a blind piano tuner, and he couldn't. It just wouldn't work, not for him. And now he was one of the sightless, struck blind in the wilderness, no help anywhere to be found, lying at the bottom of a cascade of slick but bumpy rock.

Rock. Wait a minute. Fargo stuck his hand over his head. Just air. He checked his footing, as best he could, and stood. Just as he started the last phase of straightening, his head bumped into a rock. His hands explored it. It covered him. It covered everything. There was no sky above, just rock.

The sickening realization slammed into Fargo's stomach, and he sat back down. He didn't know whether he was blind or not, but he was sure as hell inside the cave. He was still groggy as he fought off a shivering attack of panic. He was buried alive.

As a cold tremor gripped his gut, Fargo tried to concentrate on figuring out how this must have happened.

He and Jean had been at the mouth of the cave, she outside, he still in the little chamber. The two men had appeared, taking her hostage and slamming him with the Sharps, knocking him cold. They must have rolled him back into the cave. Just behind the chamber, the passage went down with a fearsome slope—they must have heaved him down that passage, then proceeded along their way back to camp, where they could take turns with Jean until they tired of her and killed her.

That galled Fargo. He reminded himself that anger seldom helped, unless you were right in the middle of a brawl. But his other choices were despair and panic, so he allowed his rage to build.

Then he dissipated some of it with a long stream of curses. At least his voice and hearing worked, for there were occasional echoes, depending on which way he had his head turned. All sorts of previously unnoticed sounds began to dominate his consciousness. Dripping water, each drop plunking like a cannon's detonation. Running water, muffled and far away, that began to rush like a waterfall. The groans of Mother Earth as her rocks adjusted to water and weather, turning into shrieks and screams of a fury bent on crushing this unwelcome invader.

Fargo wanted to plug his ears, to ignore these doleful sounds that kept getting worse. He still wasn't sure whether his eyesight worked or not, but what difference did it make here? He couldn't see, and there was nothing he cared to hear. Why hadn't they just killed him?

Or maybe they had, and this was the passage to hell, that deep place where sulfur burned eternally. No, that couldn't be right. The road to hell was supposed to be wide and paved with good intentions, not a narrow channel that was paved with slick rock. Some of Fargo's good humor returned as he decided that if he'd gotten in here while unconscious, he could certainly get out of here, now that he was able to move and think.

He had arrived here by rolling and sliding down. So it made sense to go up. The entrance had to be up there somewhere.

The cave floor tilted at an angle impossible to guess without a better grip on his bearings. He could tell up from down, more or less, and the cave floor had a tremendous slant, steep as a ladder. Its surface was damp, not really wet. The rock was smooth, although its surface undulated, and if there were crevices for handholds or projections for some footing, Fargo couldn't find them. He'd have to lie belly-down, exerting pressure every way he could, in order to keep from slipping back. It wasn't as though he had much choice, however, so the Trailsman began the toughest climb of his life.

The passage soon became even steeper. Fortunately, it narrowed, to where the walls were within reach. By jamming his feet against one wall and his shoulders against the other, he could hold his place and with considerable writhing effort gain a few inches with every wriggle.

He had no idea how far he had gone. He gasped for breath, and stinging sweat poured down his face, with only the hint of a breeze for relief. Then the walls spread, as though he had been climbing up the neck of a funnel and had reached the conical part. Belly to the rock, arms and legs spread, Fargo continued his grueling climb.

His equilibrium had been disturbed and every inch he gained required profuse straining effort. It was just a feeling he had that the slope had become even steeper, if that were possible.

It was his forward hand, the right one, that began to slip, almost imperceptibly. There was no room for mistakes here. Every taut muscle had to be strained to the utmost to keep him in place. Without the support of that hand, his body began to sag back. Almost as quickly as he could realize what was happening, Fargo felt himself slipping backward, his shirt riding up as the cool rock rubbed against his belly, his arms thrashing and his toes trying to dig down into an unyielding surface.

He barely slowed down even as he reached the narrow spot. His spread hands and legs provided some friction, but he hardly felt in control. He was bound for where he had been when he started this climb, and there wasn't a thing in the world he could do about it. If a man had let himself down with a rope, he'd have a chance of returning. But without that, it was about the same as being thrown down the shaft of a mine that had neither hoist nor ladder.

Once his wits had settled and he caught his breath, Fargo probed his stopping place. It would probably become his grave, but he tried to push such thoughts out of his mind by staying busy, and this was the only thing he could think of doing.

Okay, the chute he'd slid down ended at a rock wall. That wasn't the end of the cave, however, because those sounds of dripping and running water certainly hadn't come from where he'd been. So there had to be more cave down here somewhere. Which way? There seemed to be rock everywhere he stuck his hands, though sometimes he had to edge over a yard or two before he found a wall.

Fargo experimented with sound. In only one direction, to his right, was there any kind of echo. It was muffled, but there had to be an opening over there that would let sound through and back. And it did seem that the air was better down here than it had been farther up.

Groping that way, Fargo rounded a rock projection and found a jumble of rocks that must have fallen from the ceiling. Just the thought of any more falling rocks made him shiver, which was easy enough anyway, because this cave sat above timberline, where the air was always cold and thin.

He probed at the pile, which extended above his head. This would be easier to climb than the chute, and he didn't have anything else to do anyway.

If the rock pile had been a flight of stairs, he guessed he had climbed seven or eight steps when he felt a whiff of air wafting onto his face. It was welcome, even though it was stale. Guided mostly by the tiny air current, the Trailsman worked his way atop this pile of sharp-edged rocks. At the top the echoes started to sound normal. He guessed there would be a chamber above him, where the rocks had been, and when the resonations continued, he decided there was a fair-sized chamber on the other side. Which was as good a place to go as any.

Clambering down in the total darkness involved a few scrapes and bruises, but they almost felt comforting. They were real sensations, feelings he could trust, not like this world he couldn't see, where the sounds were coming at him from unknown directions.

There were more sounds over here: water dripping. The floor was level, or close enough not to matter. Guided by his ear, Fargo found the place where water fell, drop by drop, from the ceiling, and caught them patiently with his open mouth until his throat no longer burned.

A man could live for quite a while if he had air and water. Neither was much to brag about, but this was as comfortable as Fargo would get for a while. He curled up for a nap, or maybe a full night's sleep. There was really no way to tell. Time had absolutely no meaning down here.

When he woke up to another dark day of this continuing nightmare, Fargo stretched as was usual. His hand brushed against something that didn't feel like the usual limestone and rock. Metallic, maybe. But not like any metal he carried.

His fingers traced along the cold metal. It felt like a piece of light chain, but there was more to it, as if a lot of little chains had been woven. Nothing familiar came to mind, but Fargo knew that whatever it was, it was some indication that other people had been here before, which gave him a soaring hope that there was indeed a way to get out of this cave. Maybe there was more metal here, something he could use for tools to probe into tiny rock crevices for a grip so that he could claw his way back up that steep chute.

Now, above the woven chain, he felt something more solid. It extended upward for a foot or more, with occasional small protrusions that must be rivets. It was rounded at the top, and Fargo just waved upward, lifting his hand to mop his face, when he hit more metal. Two pieces of metal, joined at some kind of pivot or hinge. And this, too, was rounded toward the top, though there was a ridge or something sticking out.

Not accustomed to figuring out metallic shapes by the feel—he was more accustomed to the pleasant way women felt in the darkness—Fargo sat back and thought about what he might have before him. Some kind of machine, perhaps? All that he could think of that might be in this cave would be that rumored gold, and whatever was next to him, it wasn't gold bars. He reached out again.

His fingers slid into what seemed to be holes in a surface of thin, brittle rock. Fargo sprang back. Suddenly it came to him. The only conquistador's outfit that Fargo had ever seen had belonged to a Cheyenne brave who went by the name "Iron Shirt." But he remembered some pictures. The iron shirt covered a man's torso. Beneath it and extending over his arms as well as downward was a coat of chain mail, which had to be what he had felt at first. The other rounded metal had to be the helmet, which sat atop a dead man's head. Fargo realized he had just stuck his fingers into the eye sockets of a man who had been sitting here for the past eighty years, or more.

Further probing confirmed that the Spanish soldier was sitting against the wall, legs stretched out before him. The man's hands had been at his side. Next to one was a fist-sized rock, rougher and denser than the cave rocks. Fargo traced along the sharp curves of its broken edges and realized it was a chunk of flint. Strike some iron against it, and you'd make a spark.

Rather than disturb the armor, Fargo used his own belt buckle. It was as if the stars had emerged in all their glory, for an instant, as bright spots jumped from his hand. He didn't know whether to feel relieved that he still had his vision, or to feel even more trapped—this man was stuck here, and Fargo didn't know of any way out.

But he decided he had found the worst thing that the chamber would offer, so he continued to explore it, by sound and by feel. It was hard to keep his bearings—twice he found the rockfall that he had clambered over to get in here. After perhaps an hour, he knew where a level passage left this chamber, and he had found the reason why so many people had been killing and dying in this country: five heavy bars, each about the size of a common brick, lay about a yard from the dead man's left side.

Fargo couldn't see their luster, but he knew they had to be gold; nothing else that size would be nearly as heavy. It was unmistakable.

For a few minutes, Fargo allowed himself to savor the wealth that he had in his grasp. Each bar had to weigh about a hundred pounds. A quarter-ton of gold, with each ounce worth twenty dollars. That would be about a hundred and sixty thousand dollars, when five dollars a day was a premium wage, in a land where men could be killed so that the murderer could walk away in a new pair of boots. Any dream he had ever had, he could buy with this mass of gold.

But Fargo left those dreams. He'd be glad to trade all that useless wealth for a fifty-cent lantern, a tin of coal oil, a box of lucifers, and a ham sandwich. Or anything edible; his stomach was starting to grumble, reminding him that it had been at least a day since his last meal.

He fought his hunger by thinking about something else. He couldn't see any tracks, but he was the Trailsman and he ought to be able to figure out how to get out of here.

Nothing he had discovered changed the story he had heard from Darío Gallegos, so it was entirely possible that the tale was true. Spanish soldiers, pursued by Comanches, had been trying to get over the mountains, down to the San Luis Valley, where they might find some help.

Burdened by the gold, they had decided to cache it.

At least one had lived to tell the tale, so he couldn't be the man who shared this chamber with the Trailsman. What about him? How had he got there? Why was he there?

Five hundred pounds was more than any man could carry at once. So there must have been several trips, using a rope up that steep section for the returns. And then, as this soldier came back after his last trip, the outside man had taken off, with the rope. This poor bastard was stuck down here with the gold, guarding it for eternity, or at least until Carlos Hernández could return.

That wasn't real comforting. But Fargo was sure that the cross on the old parchment map was farther down the mountain. That could be explained by someone's slipping memory, perhaps, but there could be other theories.

Suppose there was a lower entrance to this cave; most limestone caves had multiple openings. Now suppose the men had come in that way, which might be more level. In which case, this man could have just been murdered, plain and simple, so that Hernández wouldn't have to share with anybody.

Fargo decided to learn everything he could from this dead man. If the deserting soldier had come down the same way he had, his armor would be banged up considerably. Instead, it had a few dents, but generally, it was in good condition. With more exploring, he found definite evidence that the man's skull had been cracked. Perhaps Hernández, the former priest, had put the man's helmet on after he gave the man his last rites.

Satisfied that there was another way out of here—or at least that there had been one—Fargo felt his way along the wall to the level passage that left this chamber. He left the gold, but he took the flint, just in case he found something remotely flammable.

The farther he went, twisting and ducking and hoping he wouldn't be forced to crawl, the wetter the walls got. Soon he was splashing on the floor, and from the noise, he could tell that there was more water ahead.

Three more rockfalls blocked his way, but only the third was a real problem. It took at least two hours of sweating labor to open a passage at its top; every time he moved a rock, more seemed to tumble down. Several banged into him. One smashed a finger. After getting past it, he felt the rush of real air, outside air, and knew he had to be getting closer.

Thus encouraged, Fargo struggled on. The first glimmer of light was so faint, yet so bright, that he wasn't sure whether it was real, or whether he really had lost his mind during this ordeal in the darkness, with his strength ebbing because he hadn't eaten in what seemed like years.

But it just had to be real. A pinhole overhead. Distances like that were impossible to judge—distant stars often looked close enough to grab—but it was well out of reach. The echoes from Fargo's hoarse shouts indicated that this chamber rose at least thirty feet over his head.

His constant companions down here, and persistent enemies, were despair and panic. Despair would make him just give up and lie down somewhere and wait for merciful death to arrive. Panic would make him thrash about uselessly, wasting energy and time; although time in the sense of hours meant nothing, he could almost feel himself shrinking as the lack of food took its toll.

Stop and think. Think about the immediate situation that he could do something about, not the gloomy prospects.

The men who had brought the gold had come this way, he decided. Had they let themselves down on ropes or ladders from that opening, far above his reach? Should he be looking for a rope or ladder? And . . . wait a minute. That water continued to flow here; it wasn't piling up. The water had to be going out somewhere. Time to explore some more.

The tiny spot of light above him provided no illumination; the void swallowed it. Fargo stumbled about, almost directly under it. He tripped over something, grabbed it, and discovered he was holding a stick that must have fallen down the hole.

But even if he had come down quite a ways since getting shoved down this cave, he had started far above the timberline. There shouldn't be any sticks to fall down the hole. He poked around and felt more wood, most of it dry.

There was a chance he might see what he was up against, and Fargo took it. His belt knife had gone with his pistol when he had unbuckled his gun belt, but he still had the throwing knife in the shank of his boot. He eased that out and began to make shavings, working cautiously because he couldn't afford to take a chance of cutting himself, and this was tricky work in the darkness.

While grabbing the buckle of the belt that held up his trousers, Fargo felt a bulge in a pocket. It was that chunk of burned cloth he had taken out of the fire pit, and it had remained dry during his wading about the cave. It was also the perfect stuff for catching a spark and holding the tiny glow.

He wadded the cloth and placed it atop the flint. He struck it with the buckle. The fourth or fifth spark caught, with a shimmering orange spot dancing on that precious piece of charred cotton. He placed it in the pile of shavings, then bent low and blew gingerly. Moments later, flames began to dance, and for the first time in an eternity Skye Fargo could see the world around him.

This had been the entrance the conquistadors had used, because the remnants of their ladder were scattered all about. When Hernández had left, clambering up to that tiny hole, he had just shoved the ladder down, and it was still here. It wasn't much of a ladder, a thirty-foot-long chunk of lodgepole, notched for climbing. One broken-off splintered piece had provided fuel for Fargo, and he hoped the rest of it would carry him to the outdoors. Otherwise, he'd have to follow the water on out, and water could flow through holes that were much too small for a man to squeeze through.

Speaking of which, that hole above looked much too small, too. But the pole caught against the rock up there, and Fargo clambered up it.

Near the top, he realized that the reason the hole looked so small was that the passage twisted so much. It was actually big enough for a man to work his way through; he could see that much as he reached the top.

His hand was leaving the comfort of the pole, going for a rock projection, when the ladder began to quiver, then tremble. Damn! He thought he'd set it down solidly, even to the extent of chocking its base with some rocks. But it was shaking now, and Fargo forced himself up one more notch and flung up both hands, grabbing at anything that felt solid.

There, he had it, even as the ladder was beginning to sway away from his body. For an agonized moment, he was suspended by his arms, his life hanging by how well he could grip with strength that was much less than normal, and ebbing by the minute. Tremors swept his body as he willed his hands into pulling himself up.

His knee brushed something solid, and that gave him the leverage to scramble further, poking his head forward, pulling his body afterward. Now there was light, welcome flooding sunlight, but he was still shaking like an aspen leaf caught by an early blizzard. No time to worry about that, just bull through, toward that light, as heedless as a moth drawn to a candle.

It was only when Fargo snaked out the opening and lay prone, gasping and panting and blinking from all that sunshine, that he realized that he wasn't the one doing all the quivering here. The goddamn ground was shaking; he could hear rocks starting to crack and slide up above.

He wasn't in the best place for that, where he might get pitched back down into the cave. He rolled away, then dizzily got to his feet, looking about for his bearings. A short limestone wall shielded the cave's opening, and it, too, sported the Maltese cross of the conquistadors, in faded red. Up on the talus slope, a cascade of loose rock was coming this way. Fargo stumbled away, trying not to trip and get caught in it.

When he looked back, after the overwhelming grinding clatter of the avalanche had passed him, the world had settled down. And the lower entrance to the cave of gold was utterly covered by a rock slide.

12

At timberline, where the bare and shattered gray rocks met the first of the trees, spruces and firs that remained bushes because the savage winter winds wouldn't let them grow any higher, the Trailsman paused to drink deeply from the refreshing cool water that bubbled out of the hillside. Only later, as the shadows began to lengthen after his nap in the shade, did he realize that the spring at his side must be the water emerging from that cave of gold and death.

He scanned the barren slope that loomed above him. The bottom entrance to the cave, the only practical way to the gold, was blocked by the tons of rock that had slid down the mountain when the earth shook. From Fargo's vantage, the upper entrance appeared to have remained open, although in the shadows, he couldn't be sure, and he had no desire to go back up there.

His stomach was growling, his battered body achingly protested even the slightest of motions, his only tool was a slender and brittle throwing knife, he was alone in hard country where people would probably continue to try to kill him . . . and he felt wonderful as he exulted in the bright sky and fresh air. Anything had to be an improvement over that cave.

Daylight was waning. This was the time when the animals stirred, when a man could club a cottontail, build a small fire, and cure his hunger. Then . . .

then, what? Fargo shook his head as he got to his feet and began staggering downhill, lurching from tree to tree. Find those bastards that had thrown him down into the cave, and if Jean was still alive, get her back from them. Fargo's anger grew with every step.

After twenty minutes of unsteady stepping, Fargo had found his spot, a tree-lined meadow where there had to be rabbits scampering about. As he looked for a suitable club among the deadfall, his sensitive nostrils detected the scent of fire. Not an active fire, but the dull odor of a drowned campfire, downstream a little ways.

Moving as warily as he could—it was hard to step lightly when taking any kind of step at all was so much work—he approached the spot. It was a small clearing, twenty yards away from the creek. Bootprints amid the trampled grass showed that it had seen recent use. There were also the prints of muleshoes and impressions from the distinctive caulking on his Ovaro's shoes. This was where Pieter van Hoorn and the other man must have been camped. Fargo peered upward. The pass that he and Jean had come over was clearly visible through a gap in the towering firs. To his right, he heard a whimper, the kind a hurt rabbit makes, and he wasn't about to argue with his belly when it told him to hurry over there.

The shadows were so deep that it took him a bit to realize that he wasn't staring at a rabbit. In a shallow grass-lined depression, Jean lay before him. Bedraggled, smudged, naked, and bruised, she shuddered with her every breath.

Fargo's first instinct was to pick her up, to hold her and comfort her. But that's all either of them would get from that: about ten minutes of comfort before the night chill settled and the bears and mountain lions began their hunting. They both needed food and warmth. Maybe this wasn't the most sensible place to build a fire, but Fargo didn't see that they had much choice.

First he clubbed a cottontail, and after skinning it, he put flint and steel to work on a fire. As the aroma of warming meat began to waft from the smoky fire, Fargo brought the slight woman closer.

He lay her on a mattress of gathered grass, then shed his shirt for some cover and used more grass for the rest. He was chomping down on a rabbit leg when she screamed.

"No, no, no more. I've told you everything." The shrieks echoed off the cliffs, blending into a wail before trailing off.

Fargo was mindful to step around and approach her from the side away from the fire, so that she could see his face and realize that he was not just a big shadow advancing upon her.

"Jean, it's me," he soothed. "Skye Fargo."

"No, no, don't lie to me," she rasped. "You're dead. I saw them kill you, throw you down the cave. You're not Skye. You helped kill him. Don't hit me again. I told you he had the map. That is the cave. There's a cross by the hole. It's faded, but you can see it. Go, look . . ."

Fargo knelt by her side. "Jean, look at me."

"No." Her blackened eyes got even more scrunched as she closed them tighter. "Do what you want to me. You're big enough to have your way, but you can't make me look at you."

The Trailsman sidled back until there was a tree trunk to lean on. He tried to sort things out.

Van Hoorn and the other man obviously weren't here now. But what had happened since he'd seen them?

They must have camped here, or close by. They knew the stories about the cave of gold, and they must have been looking for it. Fargo and Jean, both part of a survey crew that could disturb their search, had happened along. He tried to forget about his time in the cave, and study on what had happened to Jean.

They had taken her to camp and then took turns

abusing her. Then, when she was used up, they had departed, perhaps inspired by the trembling of the earth this morning. But she had told them how the cave up on the mountain coincided so closely with the cave on Fargo's map.

"What would I do in that situation?" Fargo muttered. He savored some more meat and pondered as he chewed. Two men wouldn't be enough to tackle that cave with any hope of returning as rich men, so if they had allies, they'd go get some help.

Okay, they had gone. They had probably left earlier today, while Fargo had been napping, but they would be returning. Where would they go to round up some help?

The Espinoza ranch, Fargo realized. It was the key to everything. He started putting pieces together.

María Teresa Espinoza, the woman at the Bent's Old Fort who'd lured him into the old badger game, and Ramón, if indeed that man had been her husband, were the sort of people who'd do most anything for some easy money.

But what about Pieter van Hoorn? Wait, hadn't Darío Gallegos said something about the Espinoza grant?

Right. He had heard that a foreign syndicate—it could be Dutch—had an option on buying the grant, all six hundred square miles of it, more or less. Just how big it actually was would be settled by the survey.

But why go to such work to stop the survey? That's what wasn't adding up. To delay the sale of the grant, maybe. The idea had to be to get the gold before the grant could be sold to foreign investors. That way, van Hoorn, a two-faced agent for those investors, would still get his commission on the sale, and the Espinozas would get some gold as well as their share of the sale proceeds.

The Dutch investors knew that the precise boundaries were still uncertain. So they would wait until the survey was finished. If the current survey were delayed, then van Hoorn and the Espinozas would have that much more time to find the gold from an obscure map.

Even without the map, though, they now knew where the gold was.

Fargo wanted to concentrate on what they would do about that, but Jean was moaning again amid her shivers and shudders. He managed to get a hand on her forehead before she snapped at him angrily.

"Get your hand off me," she commanded.

Fargo surprised her by doing just that.

"You want something to eat?" he inquired softly.

"Then it is you?"

"Last time I checked." The Trailsman chuckled.

"I'm sorry, Skye," she sobbed as she reached for his hand. "This is all such a nightmare . . . "

"Don't worry," he consoled. "You've got to eat something."

She opened her eyes wide and looked up at his face, barely illuminated by the flickering orange light of the small fire twenty feet away. "Skye, have you seen yourself?"

"Not many mirrors hereabouts."

"You look horrible. You're all scratched and bruised." No wonder she'd been so frightened earlier and hadn't recognized him. "What happened to you in the cave? How did you get out?"

"I found a way. The way that was on the map. Except no one will ever use it again. That slide this afternoon took care of that." He paused. "Now, sit up and eat something."

Jean bit daintily at first, then became downright ravenous. In ten minutes, there wasn't enough left of the rabbit to interest a hungry vulture. Every bone was picked clean and most had even been cracked for their marrow.

"Where are they now, Skye?" Jean wondered as he settled back.

"I thought maybe you'd know." He shrugged. "You

were around where you might have overheard them. Me, I don't even know what day it is—I've lost total track of things. For all I know, I was in that cave for twenty years."

Jean shuddered for a bit, her eyes clamped shut, and she grimaced. "Three days, Skye. Three days they had me here. They left this morning because they thought I was used up and about to die anyway. The short one said I wasn't even worth a bullet."

"Where were they going?"

"To the Espinoza ranch. They're coming back tomorrow with men and ropes and lanterns. I heard that much. They're going to get that gold." She caught her breath. "You actually saw all that gold?"

"No," Fargo explained. "It was blacker than you can imagine in there. I felt it, that's all. But I know what I held—gold's one of those things you can't mistake."

Jean's mind was racing now. "We can't stay here if they're coming back." She looked down. "I've no clothes." She examined him. "You have no weapons. They turned your horse and the mules loose."

"They probably thought that the Utes would grab the animals, and since they're the world's leading horse thieves anyway, then nobody would be the wiser about what happened to us," Fargo surmised.

"But what are we to do? Where can we go? We have nothing and we're in the middle of nowhere?"

"Look, whatever problems we have, we're both better off than we were this time yesterday," Fargo grunted. "They're not worried about either of us being around to bother them. They know where the gold is. They'll come and get it. The only question is whether anybody else happened upon those three dead surveyors at Duck Lake. If Fort Garland actually sent out some soldiers and if anybody can read sign, then van Hoorn and his buddies just might have to fight their way out of that ranch."

Jean nodded, then froze.

Fargo heard the slight sound, too. Just a rustle, and it might not mean anything more than a doe getting another bite of grass. He wished that the crackling of their fire would quiet, so that he might catch any other sounds that might be out in the gloomy void that surrounded them.

An owl hooted and another responded. His time in the cave had sharpened Fargo's hearing, and he could tell that the sound was coming from a low place, not high in a tree where owls preferred to perch. Shit. The sound was a good thirty yards away, but Fargo didn't relish the prospect of just sitting there and waiting for the Utes to close in.

Plains Indians seldom attacked at night. Part of it was that they thought night fighting was bad medicine, but the main reason was that they did most of their battling with weapons you had to aim from a distance—arrows, lances, and the like. Those were worthless in the darkness. The Utes had nothing against using arrows or lances, but they didn't mind coming right up on an enemy with a knife or club, either. So darkness didn't delay them when they were wearing war paint.

By now the supposed owl was only fifteen yards away, and the Trailsman moved away from the fire at right angles to the sound. As soon as he was in the trees, he shed his boots.

Moments later, there was one surprised Indian whose neck was caught in the crook of Fargo's elbow. The knife tip brushing against his broad, flat nose discouraged him from struggling. It wasn't until they returned to the fire, with Jean gasping but not hollering anything, that Fargo recognized his captive—Chief Ignacio.

"I thought you were my brother now and we would not shed each other's blood," Fargo whispered into the man's ear, only an inch or two from his lips.

"I believed that the Trailsman, the man who might have been my brother if his skin had been brown like mine, I believed that the Trailsman had died," Ignacio responded. "His pinto horse was not with him."

So the Ovaro, the mules, and perhaps some gear were with the foraging Utes, wherever the main band was. "How far is your camp, Ignacio?"

"A short ride in the light. Lame Otter and I saw your smoke against the night sky and came up to see if there were more horses."

The annual fall trading fair in Taos was coming, and Ignacio wanted to have lots of horses and captives, especially women, who were as good as gold there. Fargo decided an appeal to the chief's greed would work best.

"Ignacio, men will be coming tomorrow with more horses. I will help you get their horses if you give us ours back, and our gear."

"What if I do not help?"

"Then I'll see how much respect I can get from the others in your band when I walk into their camp toting your scalp."

Ignacio tensed with thought, then relaxed. "As you say, Trailsman. I think my people would fare better if you were our friend, not our enemy."

Fargo felt a lot better once they arrived at the Ute camp. Some of the younger braves seemed sullen about turning over the plunder from the mules and Fargo's saddlebags, but they trusted his and Ignacio's joint promise that there would be more tomorrow—with the further benefit that tomorrow's stuff would not inspire the unwanted attention of the Blue Sleeves. Besides, the Utes had hot stew—Fargo couldn't recognize the meat, even though he gallantly told Jean that it was beaver tail.

She seemed more comfortable in a beaded doeskin dress and elkhide moccasins with long leggings that almost reached her knees; now it was hard to see how she had ever managed to pass as a man. But the clothes didn't change her mind; she insisted on staying right at Fargo's side, even when they held the war council. Ignacio groaned that no woman had ever visited such a sacred proceeding, but conceded that it was probably all right, since Jean was too pale to be a real woman. Jean remained silent as Fargo and the Utes made plans well into the night.

The brilliant sun had climbed fairly high, although the thin air still held a morning chill as Fargo stood, stretched, and settled back down, hoping he'd find a comfortable perch.

Down amid the trees, two dozen Ute warriors were holding their horses. Hidden amid high boulders, Fargo sat at Jean's side. She was holding the Ovaro and one mule; working with the Utes was one thing, but trusting them to remember to return his horse was stretching matters long past common sense.

About an hour before noon, the awaited procession reached the pass. Fargo studied them carefully: Only van Hoorn's most trusted confederates would be along on this trip.

Tall, harsh-faced, and blond, Pieter van Hoorn led the way, atop a sleek roan that should make any horse-stealing Ute's pulse quicken. Behind him rode Ramón Espinoza. Then came two men he didn't recognize; they were dressed like ranch hands. A string of six wiry mustangs followed. They carried packsaddles, but from the way they stepped, only two were burdened with tools or gear. The others were free to tote gold in their canvas panniers. Bringing up the rear was the man who had helped van Hoorn in capturing Jean and shoving Fargo down the shaftlike entrance to the cave of gold.

Some chatter floated up Fargo's way: He couldn't make out distinct words, but from the light tone he could tell they had no idea they were riding into a trap. All Fargo had to do was sit and wait and watch the show.

Would they go for the gold first? Or would they set up camp first, so they could take their time finding the gold?

To Fargo's surprise, it looked as though they planned to do both. Van Hoorn and the rear man pulled aside at the wide spot. The others proceeded down toward the trees, while van Hoorn and his companion led their own mounts, along with the rope-toting packhorse and another one, up toward the cave.

This was going to be a long wait. The Utes were warriors, men of action prone to acts of compulsiveness and impatience, but in this case they wouldn't act too quickly. They knew that following the Trailsman's directions was the only way to gain the white men's horses without drawing the wrath of the white man's army.

It was Fargo who was edgy, impatient. Wispy clouds drifted across the blue sky, in sharp contrast to the violent storm last week. With the Utes hidden from van Hoorn and his men by banks of bushy willows, the flower-strewn meadow where the men below pitched tents seemed eerily peaceful. Fargo couldn't just sit there on this serene late-summer day with the cool mountain breeze ruffling his hair, knowing that all hell would break loose soon. Instead, he excused himself from Jean's side, telling her to stay put.

After half an hour of slow stepping among rocks that were poised to move at the slightest provocation, Fargo had worked his way down to the place where the earth's tremor had closed the second entrance to the cave. From there he scouted along the valley ridge, studying the steep slope of scree with his eagle eyes until finally he was satisfied. The Trailsman worked on around to join the Ute war party.

Noon had come and gone by the time all five of van Hoorn's party met at the upper entrance to the cave. Fargo gave the signal. Ute warriors thundered out of the willows. In full war regalia, with buckskins and feathers and laden scalp poles flying, the Utes rushed toward the ridge while launching a barrage of arrows.

It took a moment for the five white men to react, but when they did, they were predictable.

Fargo smiled as the men retreated under the overhang at the cave's mouth, the only cover available to them. He laughed at the sounds of their barking guns. Handguns. They hadn't even bothered to bring rifles.

The fury of the noise was much worse than the actual fight. The Indians hooted and hollered as they leapt from their ponies to scramble up the ridge, as adept as so many mountain goats leaping from rock to rock. Gunfire echoed across the valley. Although it sounded like a tremendous battle, no one was in any particular danger . . . yet. The Utes were still out of pistol range, so van Hoorn's sheltered men were merely wasting ammunition.

"I guess it's time to take my place," Fargo muttered to himself. He stayed out of sight as he worked his way up the mountainside. He didn't hurry. Van Hoorn and his crew weren't going anywhere.

Perched on the slope several yards above the overhang, Fargo waited until the gunfire ceased. The exuberant Utes had even settled down.

"Van Hoorn," he shouted.

"Who is that?" a voice screeched.

"Skye Fargo."

"It can't be. You're down there," someone protested.

"I got out." For once, Fargo enjoyed explaining the obvious. "And now my brothers here are going to kill all of you." He paused to let that sink in. "I just wanted you to know who sent them."

The Trailsman waited a full five cramped minutes before he stood and gave the signal. The Utes surged forward with a fresh crescendo of whoops and a new storm of arrows. From above, Jean came his way, leading the Ovaro and her mule.

Ignacio was the first Indian to emerge from the sheltered area at the cave portal. "They are gone," he muttered.

"I thought they would be," Fargo answered as he moved on to the entrance.

"They have retreated deep into the bowels of Mother Earth," Ignacio added. "Should we follow them?"

"No. What you should do is get your men, round up

your new horses, and get the hell out of here before the army arrives."

Ignacio issued those orders and turned to Fargo with a relieved smile. Fargo didn't blame him. He supposed the Utes had a few superstitions about such caves, and now that it was quieter, the Trailsman could hear why. The wind from the mountain made a strange sighing sound, like a moan.

Fargo watched as the Indians left the valley. He stepped inside the cave. On one wall of the flat landing, a chunk of iron had been jammed into a crack. A rope was tied to it; the rope went on back and down, providing the five men with their route out. Fargo pulled out his belt knife and cut the rope.

By then, Jean was at his side. "They're down there?" she whispered.

Fargo nodded. "They can stay there until the soldiers arrive."

"You're going to let the men from Fort Garland rescue them?"

"I thought so."

"Why?"

"Why?" Fargo repeated, at a loss for words.

"What happens if they're rescued, Skye?" Jean gulped a deep breath. "Van Hoorn will stand trial, and perhaps he will be hanged. But what about Espinoza and the others? What about those three dead men at Duck Lake? What can you prove about them? And how long will it take? Why don't we just leave them there?"

"But you don't understand, Jean. It's hell down there. And there's no way out. I checked earlier today."

Jean gave a cold smile. "I understand perfectly, Skye. It is exactly what they deserve."

She had a point, Fargo admitted. Once they were out, Jean could no longer masquerade as a man. She would have to testify at length to assure they were punished by the law. And there was still a good chance that some of them would get off.

"I'll leave it up to you," Fargo conceded.

"You think I'll change my mind." She raised her head to stare him right in the eye. "I shall not."

Jean glanced around the gray walls that surrounded them, then turned and fled. The Trailsman was right behind her. She didn't stop at the bottom of the slope. She paused only to mount the mule. "I want to get out of this place," she explained.

Fargo got aboard his pinto and rode beside her. The sun was beginning to set. The jagged peaks that rimmed the valley were bathed in the peculiar crimson that gave this range its name, the Blood of Christ Mountains. It was a scene of breathtaking beauty, but Fargo couldn't remember ever having felt so glad to leave any place.

Not until they had ridden for better than an hour, cresting the pass, did either of them speak. "We'll rest when we get a little lower," Fargo advised.

The moon was full, the sky retained a blue tinge, and Fargo could see Jean's smile clearly. He knew exactly how she felt. The air felt fresher and the night looked brighter on this side of the pass.

"You know, Fargo"—she laughed—"you said you couldn't relax without a woman in your arms and a featherbed under you. I do hope you'll be able to manage without the featherbed tonight."

BE ON THE LOOKOUT!

The following is the opening section from the exciting new Western series from Signet, *Canyon O'Grady*, on the stands now:

Canyon O'Grady #2
SILVER SLAUGHTER

1859, the Territory of Kansas between the Missouri border and the Flint Hills, a land seething with the rage of the red man and the schemes of the white. . . .

"Now, that's a bit of a strange one," the tall, muscular man muttered, his eyes on the road below as he sat astride the pale bronze horse with the blond mane. A two-seat Spring wagon rolled along under his gaze, one man driving, a second man in the rear seat beside a young woman. Nothing unusual there, he had first decided, and then noticed that the young woman was bound hand and foot. The tall man on the palomino had peered harder and saw she was also gagged with a thick, wide kerchief.

He ran one hand through his thick, flame-red hair, and his lips pursed as his snapping blue eyes continued to peer down at the wagon below. "I'd say we ought to have a closer look at that, Cormac, lad," he murmured and edged the palomino down the slope. When he was halfway down, he realized the wagon was moving much faster than it had seemed from above, and he spurred the pale bronze horse into a trot, cut across the slope, and headed downward again to reach the road just as the wagon rounded a curve. The driver reined to a halt as the big man on the palomino blocked his way.

"Afternoon, gents," the big, redheaded man said affably. "The name's Canyon O'Grady." He took in the two men with one quick, practiced glance. The man holding the reins was a broad figure with a thrusting jaw, the second man thinner of face and build with a three-day stubble and a long, hooked nose. Both men wore wariness on their faces at once. "I saw you from the slope," Canyon O'Grady said, and his eyes went to the young woman. "I'm a curious man," he smiled.

"Be curious someplace else," the one holding the reins growled.

Canyon O'Grady's patient smile remained. "That'd be hard to do, seeing as you're all here and I'm here," he said. The girl wore a brown dress with a square neck, he saw, and she had a somewhat thin body under the dress but high, rounded breasts and nicely turned calves. Light brown hair, brown eyes, and a short nose was all he could see of her face behind the wide kerchief that served as a gag. "As I said, I'm a curious man and right now I'm curious why you have this lass trussed up like a pig at a barbecue," he said, his voice still mild.

"It's none of your damn business," the one with the thrusting jaw said.

"Now, hold on, Fenton, you can't blame the man for being curious," the hook-nosed one cut in, plainly anxious to avoid the possibility of trouble. "She's wanted for murder back in Nobs Corner," he said to Canyon. "Fact is, she's a desperate, rotten woman. Killed a man in cold blood, she did."

"And we're bringing her back," the other one chimed in quickly. "She took off after she'd done her killin'."

Canyon looked at the young woman, who was making unintelligible sounds under the gag, and she shook her head violently from side to side as her eyes plainly pleaded with him for help. "Why the gag?" Canyon asked mildly.

"Because all she does is curse and scream. She's got a rotten mouth. We just had to gag her," the hook-nosed man said.

Canyon's eyes returned to the young woman again, fixing on the brown eyes that stayed round with pleading. She continued to make muffled sounds of protest under the kerchief. "You lads deputies?" he asked, bringing his gaze back to the two men.

"That's right," the one holding the reins snapped, and then, catching the big red-haired man's gaze, added, "We don't bother with badges in Nobs Corner."

"I see," Canyon said and saw the man beside the girl catch hold of her as she twisted and tried to fall from the wagon seat. "Well, I'm not one to interfere with deputies carrying out the law." He smiled and heard the stifled shouts from behind the gag. "Good day to you, gents," he said pleasantly and ignored the girl as she twisted and writhed with frantic desperation. He turned the palomino, crossed the road, and disappeared into the trees on the other side. When he was deep enough in the woods, he halted and peered back to watch the wagon roll on again, the driver snapping the reins hard over the horse.

Canyon ran one hand along the warm powerful neck of the pale bronze horse. "I've a bad odor in my nose," he murmured. "Let's follow along a spell, lad."

Staying in the trees, he began to follow the wagon which stayed on the road for another half mile or so and then abruptly turned off onto a steep hillside. Canyon stayed back in the trees as he climbed after the wagon and watched it struggle up the steep grade. He moved to the right as he followed and spurred the palomino on a little faster as the wagon reached a high ledge of relatively flat land. The man at the reins drove the wagon hard along the ledge, then suddenly made a half circle and turned the horse to face the edge of the ledge, where he reined to a halt. Canyon spurred the palomino higher up on the hill and halted where he could look down on the wagon and the ledge. A furrow dug into his brow.

The wagon had halted with the horse facing a sheer drop of hundreds of feet into a rock-filled gorge below. As Canyon watched, still frowning, the two men climbed from the wagon and the driver, Fenton, began to unhitch the horse. When he finished, he drew the horse to one side and returned to the wagon, where the hook-nosed man had already started to put his shoulder to the rear wheel. Canyon instantly spurred the palomino forward as one hand went to the holster at his side. But he halted still out of view as Fenton paused and stepped back.

"Wait, we've got to untie her. Can't have her found all tied up," he said. He climbed into the wagon and, drawing a skinning knife from his pocket, he cut the young woman's bonds. She erupted and tried to leap from the wagon, but the hook-nosed one caught hold of her, punched her in the stomach, and she fell back with a gasp of pain. Canyon saw the kerchief come loose to reveal full lips and a nice chin, albeit a shade thin.

"Bastards," she flung out at the two men. She tried to leap from the wagon again, but Fenton caught her, knocking her back in with a sharp slap.

"Wait. Let's enjoy her first," the hook-nosed one said. "Shit, there's nothin' to lose by it."

Fenton paused, his eyes on the young woman. "Why not?" he said. As a grin spread across his face, he reached up and yanked the girl from the wagon. The hook-nosed one pinned her arms behind her on the ground, and Fenton tried to pull her dress up. She managed to twist and Fenton took a kick on the side of his leg. "Hold her, dammit," he barked as the girl continued to twist and kick out. He caught one of her legs in his hands, twisted it, and she cried out in pain as he managed to push her dress up. Canyon got a glimpse of nice calves and round knees as she continued to kick and writhe. "Enjoy it, bitch. It's gonna be your last lay," Fenton snarled, yanking the front of his Levis open. He lowered himself to his knees over the still struggling figure of the girl, pushed her legs open with his body, and clawed at her underclothes.

"Time to interrupt the party, one-sided as it is," Canyon muttered and spurred the palomino closer. Both men were too intent on their pleasures to hear him, and as he neared the ledge he swung from the horse, landed silently on the balls of his feet, and ran forward. He drew the big Colt with the ivory grips and swore under his breath as he halted, dropping to one knee. Fenton, clumsily writhing with the girl, offered a poor target. A shot could easily wind up also hitting the young woman. Canyon lifted the Colt a fraction and took aim at the man who held her arms pinned back. He fired and the man screamed in pain as he flew backward, his left shoulder exploding in a shower of blood and bone.

"Goddamn," Fenton said in surprise as he looked up and whirled from straddling the girl. He half rose, still hanging out of his pants, and yanked at his gun. The weapon never cleared its holster. O'Grady's shot slammed into his midsection and he doubled in two as he flew backward.

Canyon had dropped to the ground the moment he fired and heard the shot from the right whistle over his head. The hook-nosed man, his left shoulder a gaping red hole, lay on one elbow, but had managed to yank his gun free and he fired again from his nearly prone position. Canyon dived to one side as another shot whistled nearby and came up firing a burst of shots. The man quivered, his body bucking, and then he lay still.

Canyon rose to his feet and was beside the young woman in one long stride. He reached his hand out and pulled her to her feet. Her eyes, still wide with fear, blinked as she peered hard at him. "It's you, it's got to be," she murmured. "Red hair, riding a palomino. There can't be two of you. You're the one they're after. . . ."